100 Days

100 Days

Victor Gonçalves

ISBN-13: 978-65-00-03065-5

Cover design by Victor Gonçalves
Photograph by Jeff Turner

Campinas, SP | Brazil

ACKNOLEDGMENTS

To my teachers,
for showing me the pleasure in reading and writing.

To Carlos, Sílvia, Camila and Rodrigo.

"Life is too short to be little."

Benjamin Disraeli

CHAPTER I

New York City, 2010.

The taxi driver turned on the radio and the Dominican music started to play loud. A sound with Latin roots and hip-hop influences. The vibration of the melody agitated my spirit and I almost laughed. The style of the song didn't quite match the image of the city that I had in my mind. But it went well with the driver. Tall, dark-skinned, long dreads in his hair and a strong perfume scent, he tried to talk to me, but I was timid since I couldn't understand his accent. When he realized my struggle with communication, he increased the volume of the radio and stayed quiet for the rest of the ride. It lasted about half an hour and we passed through wide highways with lots of signs and few cars. To enter the city area, a toll cabin. And after a few more minutes riding different neighborhoods in high speed, we stopped in front of an orange six-floored building.

- Sixty-five dollars. - he said.
- Ok. - was all I could respond, paying out a one-hundred-dollar bill to him.
- Do you have the keys? - he questioned me while delivering me the change.
- No, my host asked me to call him when I arrived, and he would open the door for me.
- Does your mobile work here?
- I don't think so...

- Use mine, then. What's the number?

While I reached the paper with Robert's information, the driver awaited with the screen lit, ready to dial. After two attempts, both unsuccessful, he let it drop into the mailbox.

- Hey, dude! Here's the deal, I'm with – and paused to ask me my name – What's your name, kid?

- Vicente.

- I'm here with Vicente. Are you gonna let him in? Are you sleeping? Man, it's almost eight in the morning! Pick up!

But Robert didn't pick up.

- That's ok, I can wait in front of the building – I said. – The agreed was that I was arriving today around this time. Soon he'll be missing me and probably going out to find me.

- Ok, man! Good luck!

As soon as I stepped out of the car, I felt the cold. A temperature that I didn't expect to deal with right away, since it was autumn. I waited a few minutes standing there but no one entered or left the building. The dry air was deepening against my face while my anxiety was growing. I tried, in vain, to learn how to use the public telephone in front of a bank next to the building, following instructions that Robert had given to me in the only time we talked, via e-mail, fifteen days earlier. He had said to me that the easiest way to contact him upon my arrival was to call and collect him using a public cabin in front of his home, but obviously that wasn't the easiest way, since I've found the instructions very hard to understand and couldn't complete the call. Maybe I was tired or maybe I just couldn't focus properly. Back to the front of the building and waiting for someone to open the door I started to realize that that was a family and quiet neighborhood. The few people passing on the street and seeing that young man, with a big suitcase on his side, seated on the steps of the entryway of a home building, gently nodded with their heads saying hello. And they seemed to know each other because now and then they stopped and started a friendly conversation.

A few more minutes later, I heard a noise coming from my back, probably the front door.

- Vicente? – a masculine voice inquired.

- Hi, it's me – I turned and answered.

- How long have you been waiting outside? Come on in, it's freezing out here.

A smiling Robert greeted me. His big blue eyes staring at me sympathetically. Tough a little bit bald and overweighed he was a tall and elegant man. *He must have been a beautiful young man*, I thought to myself. His voice had a powerful tone and his speech was very cheerful. He seemed to be one of those people who never stay quiet and love to talk about everything, always very excited.

We entered the building. Six flights of stairs and we were in front of the apartment's door. The place that was going to be my home for the next one hundred days in New York.

- *You* have to open the door, for luck. – Robert said offering me the key.

I hold it for a few seconds, thinking about the importance of that ritual. I have always liked to acknowledge important passages of life with parties and special events, but usually didn't realize the small things in order to stop and feel them properly. That moment was one of them. So, concentrating my energy to make it the beginning of a new life, I turned the key and opened the door.

The apartment had a slightly sweet scent that could be felt as soon as entering the space, as if a lot of pies had been baked in the kitchen or if the laundry had just been out of the machine, still smelling of softener. I found it curious for a man of his age, around fifty years old, living alone and in Manhattan, to have a cozy home like that. At least in my mind it was curious.

- This is the living room. - Robert began to explain. - Over there is the kitchen and at the end of this hall you can find the bathroom. That door next to it is my bedroom, and this double door here is yours. Ready?

I nodded and he opened the doors, revealing a space also different from what I expected. The dark-red walls made the entire room a retro vibe. Posters of singers like Michael Bublé and Elton John, Abba's vinyl covers, and colorful abstract paints adorned the walls. On the back wall of the room two large windows made clear that a strong sun was starting to show off. *Maybe it gets warmer later*, I thought to myself. Two brown and aged-leather couches were combined with a carpet in dark brown and blue tones, creating a kind of living room next to the windows.

- This used to be my living room, that's why the sofas are here. But I believe this space looks better as a bedroom. As agreed on the accommodation contract, I put a writing desk and a chair for you over there, so you can have a study corner. An in this corner – Robert pointed to my right – you can find your bed.

The bed was actually and enormous inflatable mattress, tall as I had never seen before. Unsure whether it could really be considered a bed, I sat on it, saw that the filling system was electric, and agreed that it might actually work as a bed. A very soft one.

- Well, you must be tired of the trip, right? - said Robert. - I have an appointment now, I'm going to the neighborhood church. You are invited to go, I think you would like it, but feel free to decline the invitation.

- Yeah, I think I'm going to take a shower, get some rest, and next time I accept the invitation, okay? - I replied.

- Sure, no problem. Make yourself at home, the house is literally yours. Have a good rest! - he said, closing the door to my room.

After a few seconds, he knocked twice and opened it again.

- Hey! We can have lunch after I get back, what do you think?

- Of course! - I agreed.

And he was gone. I took the opportunity to get to know the house better, this time walking through all the rooms. The apartment looked old, but well maintained. It was full of shelves with many books, boxes and different decorative objects, which gave the place the feeling of a home with many stories. Robert had traveled a lot, according to what I had read in his file, when I received the information about my accommodation, prior to the trip. It seemed like he had brought something from every place he had been, to decorate the place. Some natural plants could be found in the bedrooms, kitchen and even in the bathroom.

I took a quick shower, still not so familiar with the bathtub in which I needed to stand to wash myself with the shower, and then went to my room. I lay down on the bed, took a deep breath in an attempt to relax, and despite the tiredness, it took me a few minutes to fall asleep.

I woke up to the sound of footsteps around the house, evidenced by the wooden parquet floor of the apartment. *Robert is back, maybe I better get up.*

I noticed a piece of paper near the door and picked it up to see what it was. A note passed underneath.

V, the mass was incredible, you should have gone. When you get up, we can go out to see the neighborhood, and then have lunch. I'm in the next room. R.

Going to mass had never been a very common activity in my life. I was raised as Catholic, but my parents were not the type who always went to church, so I was not in the habit of practicing the religion. Nevertheless, I had a lot of faith in certain aspects of the Christian and other beliefs, such as Spiritism and Buddhism. I found the invitation to commune with strangers something different from the usual, but I was willing to experience a new life, and perhaps this ritual could be part of that new life. I managed to convince myself to go next time.

I changed clothes, left the room and found Robert in the kitchen, having a cup of tea. He offered another cup to me, but I refused and poured myself a glass of water. So, we went out for him to show me the neighborhood.

The whole vicinity was, as I had noticed at first glance, not very busy. It reminded me of the vibe of the countryside cities of my childhood in Brazil, with neighbors having conversations in front of their houses, people taking their dogs for walks, small sales on street corners, and lots of nature such as grass fields and trees. There, the sidewalk was also surrounded by trees, which already displayed some yellowed leaves, due to the change of season coming. We walked a few blocks towards north, and arrived at a large natural park, with an extensive forest. Right at the entrance we were approached by two men, asking about apartments for rent.

- I know the area a lot, and let me tell you, it is an excellent place to live. - Robert said, looking very excited. - But I don't think there are many rental options available. Anyway, walk eight blocks in this direction - pointing south - and you will find a real estate company, Real Houses. Talk to Janet and tell her I sent you.

- Wow, thank you very much! - the two men thanked at the same time, smiled at each other, and headed south.

I couldn't help noticing that it was a homosexual couple, and I smiled slightly when I said goodbye. *Robert seemed so excited to help them. And the way he talked seemed different. Maybe he is gay.* - I thought. In general, when I observed someone's very positive attitude towards gay couples, I tended to think that the person was also gay. Maybe because I was raised in a country with a lot of prejudice, or secretly hoped to be surrounded by people in the same situation as me. So, Robert raised my curiosity even more.

- Did you notice anything different about those two boys, Vicente?

- How so? - I played dumb, although I did not intend to.

Robert looked at me for a moment, as if he expected me to keep talking.

- Never mind, we'll talk about it later.

I was torn between insisting that he continue or pretending that I was naïve and really didn't understand what he was talking about. I chose the second option. But with a hint of regret inside me.

Along an extensive walk through Fort Tryon Park, Robert and I talked about what I was doing in my home country before the trip, about what had led me to study English in the United States, about my expectations about the course and about the city, and about my family. I explained that I worked in Advertising, that I had just left a job in an agency and that I was venturing into the field of artistic photography. I said that I wanted to take advantage of the rest of the year - it was October - to improve my English, since I had not studied the language outside the traditional school, and I still had some difficulty with the conjugation of verbs and prepositions. About the city, I only knew it through photos and movies, and I had always been very curious to know what it was like to live on the island of Manhattan. As for my family, I started talking about my parents and my brothers, my dog, and then I missed them. I had never been away from them for a long period of time, nor traveled alone, so that would be also part of the challenge within the trip. Robert listened carefully, agreeing at times. The simple fact of having someone interested in what I was talking about, even in an unfamiliar environment, made me feel good.

We left the park and continued down a street full of colorful buildings. We stopped at a door with drawings of yellow flowers. Yellow was a restaurant during the day, and a bar at night. Its decoration was all in white and yellow, and flowers were scattered all over the tables. We sat down, and Robert continued the conversation.

- Vicente, your English is very good. Are you sure you came here to learn the language?

- In fact, I came to improve speech and writing.

- Right. And that's it?

At the time I could not confess to myself that the whole trip had been an excuse for an inner search, an escape from problems that affected me, an urgent need for change and personal growth. Let alone say all that to Robert.

- Yes, and maybe live far from where I was born and grew up, for a change. - I replied.

He was satisfied with my answer.

The waiter arrived to take our orders. We both chose the dish of the day, an eggplant salad followed by a pasta with tomato sauce.

- You know, - Robert started again - New York is a concrete jungle, as poets often joke. Speaking for myself, If I could, I would move. I am tired of here. Especially Manhattan and its central region, full of tourists, bright lights and promises that cannot be fulfilled.

Without realizing that the excited tone in his speech had given way to a certain bitterness, I was startled. I couldn't understand the negative reaction. The first one about the city I chose to spend the next three months of my life.

Why this pessimistic opinion about New York? Especially today, having I just arrived? And coming from him, who until then had seemed so happy about life? were the questions that came to my mind instantly.

I was unable to go on after his comments, so I suggested that we order a dessert. Robert accepted, and we both shared a chocolate pie. And the bill, at the end of lunch.

The rest of the afternoon was spent unpacking my suitcase and sorting my clothes and personal belongings into cabinets and shelves in my new room. I found in one of the pockets of my backpack a key-chain that I had won as a gift from a friend during a farewell party. It was a small metal Brazilian flag. I fitted the key to my new home on the keychain.

The night arrived, along with the tiredness I still felt in my body and especially in my mind, and after accompanying Robert in a potato soup he had made at home, I went back to my room to read. I fell asleep without realizing it.

The twelve months before my trip were different from the other twenty-five years of my life. I had come out of a difficult period, from unsuccessful job attempts and broken friendships, and had been experiencing a new type of semi-freedom for the first time in my life. Semi because I was living with my brothers, although having my own routine inside and outside the house. During the week, I used to work my own projects related to art and photography, and on weekends I usually went out with friends. New friends, recently conquered, who helped me discover new approaches to a world that I thought I already knew, but that due to shyness or lack of courage, I had not yet conquered. I had been learning to accept new things and places, without fear of meeting different types of people or new life opportunities.

In the midst of this new positive lifestyle, I had also found someone who made my heart beat faster than ever. My thoughts had become his every day, all day. An overwhelming, almost inexplicable
passion - except for the fact that he was everything I had dreamed of
in a man. Or almost everything, but at the time it didn't matter. Lucas and I had an affair for almost a year but had left it unfinished till
the day before my trip. Lucas was the last person to whom I had said
goodbye, in tears, towards a journey of personal discovery. And,
without him knowing it, towards a desperate attempt to forget him.

Our relationship had never been official, but it had been intense
from the beginning. Weekends at the beach, night after night going
to the movies and feeling part of the romance seen on camera, and
even plans to live together. Everything seemed better with him by my
side, and all the time I felt it was reciprocal. For a while, it was a secret, nobody knew about us, and that made everything more special.
Gradually, some friends to whom we opened the relationship started
to support us. I was so happy. I had even taken him to my parents'
house for them to get to know each other. However, in the weeks before the trip, everything got complicated. Lucas no longer gave me the
same attention as before and started to insist that we become just
friends. What do you mean, just friends? - was I incredulous - What
has changed, how do you feel about me then? - I insisted. And his
reaction was always the same: an unanswered look, a long and tight
hug, and most of the time, a night of sex. And the next morning,
strangeness would come back to attack us. Not even the announce-
ment of my trip made the situation change. I didn't want that anymore, and I decided to combine to my other trip goals the acceptance
of the idea of friendship between us and expect to return home con-
vinced that the passion was over, that our story was history.

My first thought, the morning after I arrived in the land of Uncle
Sam was that I was in a dream. I opened my eyes, looked around, and
the sunshine coming from the windows that I had forgotten to close
at night almost blinded me. It took me a while to see the room and

understand where I was and that it was all real, not imagination. It was Monday, and a national holiday in the country, Columbus Day. My classes would start the next day, so I had that one to do whatever I wanted. Including nothing at all.

The panic of nothingness started to break after a breakfast with fruits, cereals and the company of Robert who, back in good spirits, proved to be an excellent host, preparing me coffee and being a good company for conversation during the meal. In the accommodation contract, it was not required that I have a close relationship with my host, on the contrary, it exempted both parties from sharing their routines. But it was not what was happening there, perhaps due to excessive kindness of Robert, or simply because of a needy personality. He had left the house for his daily errands, and I found myself alone, having to decide what to do. It was not the first time in my life that I had found myself in that situation, but it was the first time that I had found myself in that situation outside my home, outside my country, away from my family and friends. To make matters worse, even though I was in the city I chose, in the time of the year I chose, with thousands of options to choose from, I had no idea where to go and what to do.

I started pacing, looking for a quick solution, as I had seen so many times in movies, and that had always worked for the characters. Nothing happened. I accessed the internet from an old notebook that Robert had lend me, looking for interesting attractions, but my brain couldn't absorb anything. At that moment, the memory of my life in Brazil, which I had said goodbye to just two days ago, hit me violently and I couldn't think of anything else. Then I knelt down on the floor and started to cry.

I cried for the fear of not being able to accomplish any of the goals that I had set for myself, and that at that moment were clear in my head. Forget Lucas, learn to live alone, find out who the real Vicente was. I cried for the lack of dear people close to me, some of whom I hadn't even managed to say goodbye to. I cried for the unknown that awaited me the following months. And I cried for Lucas, for the feeling I still had for him. I stayed like this for a while, waiting for the tears to stop falling, and for some courage to appear.

I heard the apartment door open, steps down the hall, and the door to Robert's room close. I thought about leaving my room and going to vent with him, but something stopped me. An uncertainty about the intimacy I would create with him, and how much our different cultures could be a barrier in this case, prevented me. I decided to get up, dry my tears and leave the house.

Just like the day before, the weather was clear but with a low temperature, which I was not used to. It was another first time for me: going out alone without destination in New York. I realized this after walking for a few minutes, heading south. Then my feet started to get heavy, I felt an anxiety take over my chest, my breath failed, and I stopped in the middle of the sidewalk. *Where do I go? -* I thought, in a hurry to get an answer. *I can learn how to ride the subway, in addition to exploring downtown Manhattan, after all I'm in New York! -* I answered excited to myself. But in a matter of seconds, this animation turned to anxiety again, and I remained still. After a few more minutes of looking at the window of a stationary store a few blocks from my new home, I decided to start slowly and get to know the surroundings first. It would be fine for now.

I had walked with Robert the previous day for a big part of the neighborhood, but walking it alone made me realize other nuances. Although quite familiar, with a predominance of elderly people, the vicinity had also young residents and immigrants. Dominicans could be found whenever loud music was heard from a car, or when women crossed the street dancing. If the whole place was a painting, it would look like colored brush strokes amid a predominance of mild and pastel colors. Drunk by the melody of the music coming from one of the cars, similar to that one in the taxi the previous day, I felt myself lighter and willing to go a little further.

After a ten-minute walk heading north, I arrived at Fort Tryon Park. The huge park, in which I hadn't entered the day before, curiously made me feel at home. Large rows of trees, the smell of grass, and several species of flowers transported me to the park where I practiced running regularly in Brazil. But the specific architecture like bridges, stairs and tunnels made it clear that this was another park. I distracted myself walking along the stone walkways and admiring the view of the Hudson River. I started to notice my breathing more relaxed. I took some pictures with my camera, and examined them on the screen, sitting on a bench. Two children were playing with wooden cars next to me, being watched by their parents on another bench. A boy and a girl. It was inevitable to remember my childhood, playing with my brothers and being cared for by our parents. That place and that scene exuded normality, and for me, nostalgia. I watched them for a while, and then I got up and continued my way. A path still without destination, but with more serenity.

The park was much bigger than I had imagined, so I took advantage of one of its exits to return to the sidewalk and continue walking through the neighborhood. I passed by churches - *I wonder which one Robert attended* - by squares where gentlemen seemed to talk and challenge each other in board games, and child schools with playgrounds on lawns outside the buildings. There was nothing there that reminded me of the metropolis I had hoped to visit when I chose New York, but still the walk made me happy, satisfied and hopeful.

I stopped at a Starbucks, on one of the great avenues that cut through the neighborhood and had a hot sandwich. The choice seemed safer, since I already knew the franchise and the food and drink options. I chose a Frappuccino to accompany me the rest of the way. Before returning to the apartment, I stopped at a market open despite the holiday. It was difficult to understand the products and differentiate them by the packaging. There were a lot of canned food, many boxes of cereal, and many dairy products. I chose some items, considering breakfast and snacks to take to school. After all, my routine plan was to leave for class early, spend all days getting to know the rest of Manhattan, and come home only at night.

Back to the apartment, my afternoon was spent watching movies on the borrowed notebook, in English and without subtitles, to improve the language. Robert arrived early in the evening and took me out to dinner at a restaurant owned by one of his friends, a cozy place with delicious dishes. We talked about my day, but he didn't tell me much about his. Before returning home, we stopped at the 181 Street subway station, the closest to our building, to buy and charge a metro card. That would be my official transportation from that moment on. We arrived at the apartment and each of us went to their respective room. I needed to sleep so I could be fresh for the first day of school the next day. The first day of the rest of the trip.

Lying in bed, in the dark, I could not escape the frustration of not being able to go further during the day, remaining only in the neighborhood. Although I thought the tour was good and that improved my mood, I wished it could have been better. I was afraid to repeat mistakes in my life. I needed to change, and that was why I had forced myself into a new pattern, a new place, a new life. The start had been given, and I couldn't quit the race.

CHAPTER II

The subway was different from the ones I had been on. It was visibly old, though well maintained and working perfectly. People did not look at each other's faces but only paid attention to their cell phones, notebooks and, in the case of some women, mirrors by which they were guided to put on their makeup. It was almost impossible to distinguish social classes in that car. Apparently, everyone was going to work or study, like me.

I got off at the 28th Street station, and immediately heard a song, as if I was arriving at a concert. I walked for a while looking for my way out to the street and saw a stunning woman singing an old Mariah Carey song. Without the equipment usually seen in professional performances, she was able to transform a small space next to the turnstiles into a stage with her singing, and the acoustics of that basement only seemed to help her perform a real show. Nothing but her, her guitar, and her magnificent voice. I put a dollar bill in a cardboard box with her name handwritten on it, Charlene, and felt like the day was starting well. For both of us.

Going up the stairs to Seventh Avenue, I instantly realized that the neighborhood was not even similar to the one I was living in, in

Washington Heights. I was in the central region of the city, in the *eye of the hurricane.* Hurried pedestrians, sirens of police cars and ambulances, smoke coming out of manholes, very tall buildings, different languages. This was the *real* New York. At least according to the movies and TV series I had watched my whole life.

Arriving in front of where my school was supposed to be, I noticed something odd on the facade. The building appeared to be under renovation, and the entrance was closed. I asked a security guard of the building for information, and he indicated the building next door as an entrance. I resumed walking on the sidewalk, and when I turned to thank him, I bumped into a girl.

- I'm sorry, I didn't see you! - I tried to ease the shock.

- No problem, it was my fault. - she said, with a gentle smile on her lips.

We both continued on our way, and surprisingly it led us to the same place.

- Are you also heading to Diplomacy School? - I asked.

- Yes! It's here, right?

- I believe so. My name is Vicente, nice to meet you.

- Clara, nice to meet you too.

- Are you two coming in? - another security guard interrupted us, opening the building's large glass door. - It is forbidden to stand in front of this building. If you are a student, please come in.

The elevator was full of other students, from different countries. When we reached the sixth floor and went straight to a reception area, we were all directed to a line that followed the walls of a long corridor with some doors open. Inside the first room our photos were taken, and instantly printed on a student ID card. In the second room we were interviewed by teachers, who rated us considering the level of English in our conversation. In the third room, they organized us in groups of fifteen students. In the fourth and last room, a written test was applied to assess our level of knowledge in grammar and vocabulary in the English language. The whole process was fun.

After the written test, we were placed in a waiting room for us to meet the school's principal. Minutes later he appeared and welcomed everyone. Then he presented us the school's history, the technical qualification of the teachers, and finally the schedule of classes and extra-school activities. Clara was seated next to me during the presentation, and at the end of it the director dismissed us, informing that classes would start the next day, at seven in the morning.

- The principal was very specific about absences, huh... - I started a conversation with Clara.

- Yes. - she laughed. - So, what level did you end up at?

- Number 6, how about you?

- Number 5. - she said, looking a little upset.

- Well, I'm sure you will soon change to the 6, and we will be in the same room. - I tried to cheer her up, and also cheer myself, after all it would be nice to have a familiar face with me during classes.

- I hope so.

A silence took us. I could not think in any topics to go on with the conversation. I thought about suggesting a place for us to lunch, but I hesitated.

- Shall we look for a place to have lunch? - Clara was more daring than me.

- Sure! - I agreed, smiling.

And we left school. I was feeling improved, more comfortable and with a possible new friend. I recalled my school days during childhood and adolescence, and how much I liked to study. I had missed this kind of social environment over the years, without even realizing it. Well, at that moment I did.

Clara opened the subway map, which we had won from the director so that we could familiarize ourselves with the city's public transportation system.

- I've always been told that I had to go to Chinatown at least one time, because of the restaurants. Apparently, they are the best for those who like oriental food - said Clara. – So, I thought about starting there. Do you like Japanese or Chinese food?

- I prefer Chinese food. - I said.

- Then we should go to this one. - she pointed out an address in her city guide.

- It works for me.

Riding the subway was not being a difficult task, and it was making me feel inside one of the many movies I had watched, in which the characters always think about life and their problems as the trains go by, and you can see all kinds of people, from the most tidy to the most exotic dressed. I was beginning to enjoy the experience. In Brazil, it was rare for me to use public transportation, since I had a car. But in New York everything seemed to happen smoothly, efficiently and safely. And Clara seemed to be willing to learn how to use that kind of transportation properly, just as I was.

We arrived at Chinatown and it seemed like another country. It was amazing how after a few minutes of traveling under the ground I felt transported to a totally different place. We found the restaurant chosen by Clara and had a delicious meal. Then we discussed going back to school to check the calendar of extra-school activities. Clara insisted that we should do the suggested activities, so we could meet new people and spend less money, since the school offered discounted tickets. We decided to take the subway halfway and walk the rest of the route. The long walk was a way to get to know each other more, and also get to know more about the city, our new home.

Clara was a young Venezuelan woman who had finished college and was working on research in the chemistry sector at a university back at her native town. She liked music, especially rock, and was living in a rented room in an apartment in Queens. She had just ended a relationship that had lasted four years, she was very close to her family - her parents, her brothers and her cousins - and she was in New York to improve her English and also have fun. And she was fun. In addition to some similarities in our lives, we had the same kind of humor and that earned us good laughs along the way.

After a brief stop at Diplomacy, we decided to keep walking and take the early evening to enjoy the view of that delightful city. For both of us, it was unusual for the sun to set early, before five o'clock in the afternoon, making way for the night. But everything was new for us, and even a longer night could make sense in that new reality. Ten blocks later, through the many lights of small shops and commercial workplaces, I noticed a strong glow coming from some buildings a few blocks away. It was not evident to me, but it looked like a clearing in the middle of many tall constructions. Two more crosswalks and we were facing a large square.

- Wow! This is amazing! - exclaimed Clara, looking at me and then up.

My mind couldn't take in the fact that this was the famous Times Square. So colorful, bright, grand and... real.

The sky could not be more beautiful, toasting the early evening with an intense turquoise blue. The buildings around it seemed to revere the open space, perfectly designed with pedestrian paths, plants in strategically located pots, and various sets of tables and chairs inviting anyone to sit and enjoy the moment. Gigantic led panels with high-resolution moving images looked extremely palpable transporting the visitors to different scenarios. Giant posters announcing musicals that promised to be *the biggest hit of the year* or *masterfully directed* set the artistic and mediatic tone of that space. The only things that made the ambiance less perfect were the smell of burning rubber, probably coming from street food carts - and the vast number of tourists.

- You know, I imagined it to be different. Maybe smaller. - I said to Clara.

- Smaller? Everything here is exaggerated, haven't you noticed yet? - she replied, laughing.

- It's true. But even so, I didn't expect it to be so full of tourists.

- Vicente, this is New York, what did you expect?

- I don't know...

- You don't know? Didn't you come here with clear goals?

- Yes, I did. But I may not have considered all aspects, I think.

- Did you come to New York because it's New York or just because it's a different place and it's far from where you lived?

We had already achieved a certain level of intimacy, but I never thought of having such a deep exchange with Clara, not at that moment. I had told her that I had reached a stage in my life where I was looking for some answers and some changes, and that I had chosen to be there with clear intentions, but I didn't go into more details. Actually, I realized that I didn't have a proper answer to her question, although she had a point. I had chosen to travel abroad to enhance myself, but until that moment I had not analyzed why New York. Maybe I had chosen to be there because I had wanted to know that place for a long time. But maybe it had been because of the references I had cultivated through books and movies, that by being there all my dreams would come true, that there I could be who I wanted to be. But were my goals necessarily related to New York, or could any other place serve me as well as that famous city?

We continued to walk and decided to enter inside an inviting deli. The place exuded different cultures, especially because of the eclectic menu and, again, different accents heard in conversations. Each table seemed to have its own language, and some of them I couldn't even identify which country was it from. We found a table near the entrance.

- You know, Vicente, I understand you. - Clara continued the previous topic.

- What do you mean, you understand me? - I asked, curious.

- You're a little bit lost. It's normal, so am I. Being in a city like this, alone, and wanting to change can be scary. The memories of our other life, the one we lived before we got here, can insist on bothering us and trying to make us give up. But we need to be stronger and learn that we can choose how to live our life.

- It's easy to say it, but hard to do it. Isn't it? - I interrupted.

- Yes, it's difficult, but not impossible.

- You're right. - I agreed.

- You're not here to forget someone, are you? - asked Clara, with an inquisitive look that I couldn't escape.

Thousands of answers came to mind, but I was unable to say them out loud. Then she continued.

- We've all had a broken heart, and believe me, I know how it is. I shared an apartment with my last boyfriend and one day he came home, told me he was in love with another person and left. That was worse than a stab in the back. Geez, I gave up a lot for him, including a good relationship with my parents, who didn't like him and didn't approve of our relationship. But I couldn't accept that everything went wrong, go back to my parents' house and live with this failure. So, I decided that no one else would have the power to make me sad or make me give up anything in my life. I just need to strengthen myself. And forget what hurt me.

I was thoughtful for a few seconds, not knowing how to proceed with the conversation. Not only did she understand what I was going through, but her situation seemed even more critical than mine. And she had said everything I was feeling inside, in just a few sentences.

The waiter arrived to take our orders and then went out to arrange them.

- I don't know about you - said Clara - but I came to New York because I received a signal. I opened a geography book, closed my eyes, and randomly pointed to a location on a world map. I opened my eyes and my finger was over New Jersey. I thought it best to drag it a little to the right, and there it was, in Manhattan. - she said, laughing.

And that laugh won me over. Although I was there to learn how to live alone and find my own way, perhaps Clara could help me with this task.

When I got home, Robert was waiting for me to find out what my day had been like. I felt like the first time I saw him, with him asking me about everything. We talked for almost an hour, during which he corrected me when I made a mistake in the pronunciation or construction of a sentence. I found it very helpful, realizing that it could help me to level up faster at school.

After a cup of tea, he excused himself and went to sleep. But first he handed me a book for me to read and improve my English. After a relaxing bath I went to my bedroom, closed the doors, and lay on my bed. I quickly leafed through the book, *Father Joe*, by Tony Hendra, and a phrase stood out on one of the pages. It said, *if a cat has kittens in the oven, are they biscuits?* That sentence sparked another reflection in my head. Clara had made me think about why I was there, apparently with mixed expectations since I was not sure about the nature of my choice. Had I deliberately chosen New York? Was I just running away from my previous life, or from myself? What's more, being far from everything would be enough to bring me any change? Would New York help me achieve my goals? What kind of transformation could I expect? It took me a long time for me to sleep.

CHAPTER III

- What would you take to a desert island, and why? - asked Thelma, my teacher.

- I think I would take with me a good book to distract me, and a lot of liquid to keep me hydrated. - I replied, looking at the other students and trying to sound wise.

The purpose of that exercise was to test our vocabulary. Classes had officially started, and it was time to learn more. My colleagues all seemed still self-conscious, like me, but over the following few hours we were interacting more with the teacher, and with each other. By the time we left, I had already made two new friends, both Japanese and both very friendly: Tanaka and Akihiro. The idiom was a difficulty to be overcome by them but somehow, we managed to understand each other and agreed to have lunch together.

To my surprise and relief, the place chosen by them was not an oriental restaurant, but instead Italian, and I was able to eat a delicious pasta with meatballs. Clara accompanied us, since she hadn't made any new colleagues in her class yet and I was her only friend. After lunch, Tanaka invited us to go to an arcade near where he was living, not far from where we were. Although electronic games had never been my forte, and neither Clara's, we decided to accept the invitation. While Tanaka and Akihiro danced incessantly on top of one of those machines that play music and shine instructions on how to move, Clara and I sat and talked, over a bowl of ice cream and peanut butter pie.

- Do you still miss home? - asked Clara.

- I haven't thought about it. - I replied.

- But it doesn't come to your mind?

- Once in a while, but I know they are well and that's enough for me, so...

- I admire your strength, you know?

- Me too, and I didn't even know I had it. - I said, smiling and realizing it for the first time. - Do you think much about your family? - I asked her.

- Yeah, a lot. I think it's because I don't have a social life here yet.

- But it's still early, we had just arrived. In time we'll build one, at least I believe that.

- I guess. - she said thoughtfully. - In the meantime, shall we make a deal?

- What deal?

- We'll keep each other company for as long as we can, and we'll not argue over silly things.

- Clara, I don't usually argue over...

- But let's make this a deal! - she interrupted me. - And let's start by doing all the touristic activities in the city, getting to know all the monuments, places that guides indicate.

- All right! - I agreed. - And how are we going to seal this deal?

- Lift your spoon. - she ordered.

I licked what was left of the mint ice cream and held it up. She then lifted her fork still dirty from the pie and hit the two handles.

- Deal! – she said.

- Deal! - I repeated. And we laughed.

The next day, after class, Clara and I went to visit the first tourist spot on our list, The Empire State. As I was used to be afraid of heights, I was curious to see if I could keep myself calm on top of one of the largest buildings on the island of Manhattan and one of the largest skyscrapers in the world. I thought the term skyscraper was funny, because it seemed impossible that a building could be so tall that it inspired that feeling. But when we arrived on the sidewalk in front of it, on Fifth Avenue, and looked up, I understood the meaning of the expression.

- Isn't that too high? - Clara looked at me, startled.

- Probably, yes! I've never been so high up. - I said, knowing that that comment could be interpreted in many ways but in my head, I was trying to depict my personal situation of never having reached so far before in life. - But if King Kong wasn't afraid, I shouldn't be, right? - we laugh.

We entered the building and a large lobby received us, with its imposing decor. A lot of golden, varnished wood and crystal chandeliers gave the building a luxurious tone. One of the employees characterized by a uniform with golden details promptly guided us to a second room, where the ticket office was located. Tickets purchased, we faced a short line and after a few seconds inside two elevators that raised us to a height of more than eighty floors, we reached the top. Like in Times Square, we could see many tourists flocked, but this time it was on four sides of a long parapet surrounding the entire building, overlooking the north, south, east and west of the island and adjacent regions. We approached one side to look down at the city and then there was no doubt: New York was fascinating. And, to my surprise, silent. When faced with the magnitude of that view, I allowed myself to hear the strength within the silence. I was able to discern the lines, the colors and the paths of the city, aspects that I was only aware of with the absence of sound. The only perceptible noise was the wind, providing even more cold up there. I contemplated the view for a long time, imagining the countless possible stories down there. Clara joined me, in silence, for a few minutes. Then, nurtured by that feeling of astonishment, and after taking a few pictures of us at that iconic place, we felt satisfied and went down.

Only when I got back to the sidewalk did I remember the fear of heights again. And the lack of it up there.

Two weeks passed, and a routine was beginning to take shape for me. During the weekdays, I was up very early, and after a quick shower and a light coffee, usually alone with Robert still asleep, I was used to spend forty minutes on the subway to get to school, where I was studying for six hours. I usually had the rest of the day free to choose what to do. On weekends, walks through different parts of the city, alone or with the company of Clara and other eventual schoolmates were the pattern.

Clara and I had already visited lots of city's main tourist spots such as The Statue of Liberty, the New York Public Library, The Grand Central Station, The Madison Square Garden, The Rockefeller Center, and The Museum of Modern Art. While we walked through the history and peculiarities of the city, we also exchanged important information about each other. I already knew that we both had a dog as a pet, that she enjoyed movie sessions with popcorn, and that she liked thin and stylish men. She already knew that my host had helped me to improve my English, that I preferred cold instead of hot coffee drinks, and that I enjoyed funny people as a companion for any type of pastime. I didn't make it clear that in terms of romantic relationships by *people* I meant *men* but apparently, she didn't think that was an important aspect. That Saturday, we were going to the Brooklyn Bridge to watch the sunset.

Since Clara was living outside Manhattan, in Queens, and I was on the northern end of the island, we had agreed to always meet halfway to go on our tours. That time was no different, we got together in Times Square, our official meeting place, and took the subway to the southern end. The weather was getting colder every day, and it was necessary to wear warmer clothes, especially after the sun went down, when an icy breeze was frequent. As we arrived at the bridge, we saw the usual large number of tourists trying to find the best angle to take pictures. Clara and I dodged the crowd, trying to find the best place to admire the sun hiding on the horizon.

While the sky was still clear, in strong shades of blue, we talked about how wonderful it was to always find, among tourist groups, people alone and thoughtful. It was common and fun for both of us to watch this type of characters and try to guess what they were thinking. What was the story behind each one of them, and why were they alone. At a short distance from us, a lady was sitting on a bench facing the side of the bridge from which The Statue of Liberty could be seen.

- This lady is in her sixties and she is in town to visit her daughter who lives here. - tried to guess Clara. - Notice how pleasant your expression is. She is happy. Earlier, her son-in-law took her and her daughter out to lunch and the lovely couple are now under the bridge, waiting in line to get a ticket to The Phantom of the Opera.

- Yes, she prefers sunsets to musicals. - I completed the description, laughing.

- Ok, now you start. - ordered Clara.

I focused on a young skater, on the other side of the bridge, leaning on the metal frame, looking out over downtown Manhattan.

- This young man had a disagreement with his parents, grabbed his skateboard and ran away. He lives in Brooklyn, and has a dream of being a famous skateboarder, but his parents don't agree with him. They think he should focus on his studies and be successful in the business world. - I analyzed the boy.

Clara added:

- And you see that other young man, next to him? See how he stares the boy. I think he likes him. - she said, looking directly at me.

Until that moment, we had talked from gastronomy to fashion, from architecture to chemistry, and even about her past relationships. But I had not felt comfortable talking about my homosexual condition. At that moment though, I felt that Clara was trying to overcome this barrier and make me reveal a part of me that she still didn't know. Before I could think of something to say to her, she continued talking.

- We've been friends for three weeks now, and I still haven't heard stories about the girls you've dated. Tell me, what's the name of your last girlfriend? – she insisted.

I didn't have any important stories about girls, and the first story that came to my mind was about Lucas. It took me a while to think about how to tell her about that, about all the issues involved in that case, having to change the sex of the person in question. I was starting to consider opening up to her, telling her all the truth she was asking for, after all she would probably understand my situation and why I hid that part of my stories. But as usual, she didn't wait for me to respond.

- There are no girls in your life, right? - she smiled kindly.

The first instinct was to disagree with her, maintaining my privacy on that matter. But that feeling lasted for milliseconds. The sky had already gone from blue to orange and yellow shades. I was overcome with a sense of openness, and couldn't have another reaction but to smile back, and nod. *Wow, this feels good.*

- I knew it! - She yelled, hugging me.

- I was gonna tell you, but I was waiting for the right time. - I felt the need to say something, trying to explain the omission.

- You were not, Vicente! If I didn't bring it up, you'd be gone in two months without telling me this. – she laughed.

- Yeah, probably. - I couldn't lie to Clara anymore.

- Well, that's awesome! Let's go out today to celebrate! In a gay nightclub! I always wanted to go to a club like that. Let's go? Please!

And I continued to agree with her, nodding my head. I was feeling light, happy, and for the first time since I arrived in the city, connected to that aspect of my life. Clara made me tell her about my old boyfriends, affairs and romances. And of course, we talked about Lucas.

Until then, I was trying to set up a new life pattern, strengthen my ties with Clara and some other colleagues at Diplomacy, have a good relationship with Robert, and feel less nostalgic about Brazil and my old life. I was preparing myself for the moment when the questions that always came to my mind before going to sleep would have to be answered. Talk about other men and look for love had been two of the main things I had done in recent times. And Lucas had been my focus for the past few months before the trip. For the first time that year I was able to focus on other matters, and that attitude was proving to be so effective that I hadn't thought about men, love or Lucas for weeks. But I relived a little bit of that as I talked to Clara.

- As soon as we've met, I realized you had an unfinished love story. - she said.

- Is it noticeable? - I asked.

- For me, it is. One broken heart attracts another. - she joked, but wisely.

I smiled at her. We had reached a new status in our friendship.

The horizon was beginning to show a beautiful deep purple on one side of the bridge while the other, with the silhouette of the Manhattan buildings, was already plunged into the night and shining with the help of a few stars up in the sky, and many lights down the city. Being up there, with the cars riding below us and the city standing miles away, seemed like a metaphor for what I was experiencing. As my new life was developing itself, I was having the opportunity to see it from afar, analyze it, and choose what I wanted from it. I just needed to see more clearly what I could do, and what I really wanted. For now, I was sure about one thing: opening up to someone else had been easier than I had imagined, and that could be the first sign of evolution. That moment deserved a celebration.

- Welcome to Splash! Love your shoes, girl! They're sickening! - the cloakroom drag queen praised the pair of heels that Clara had bought especially for the occasion.

- Thank you! - said Clara, not sure of what *sickening* meant in drag queen slang but taking it as a compliment.

She handed our coats to the red-haired *glamazon* on the other side of the counter and took two condoms from a machine by the wall, putting one in her pocket and one in mine.

- For later. - she said, blinking an eye.

- Clara, this is a gay club! What makes you think you're going to find a straight man here? - I asked, laughing at her attitude.

- It's New York, baby! Anything can happen! - she embodied her nightclub persona and dragged me dancing to the bar near the dancefloor.

We ordered two drinks, one for each, and the most beautiful waiter I had ever seen served us. We made a toast, turned the drinks and went to the dancefloor. The place was full of disco balls that reflected green and blue lights, reaching the entire space and also small lounges around it. I hadn't heard such a good setlist in a long time, and suddenly the world stopped. I don't know if it was the alcohol effect, the loud music, or just the good feeling of life without strings, but I felt myself floating. Clara and I burst into laughter, and the place suddenly became more and more colorful. People around us were very friendly and looked at us smiling. Clara was providing new drinks as soon as the previous ones were over. We toasted to the city, to the future. Suddenly, at one corner of the dancefloor, a guy caught my eye. Blond, tall, athletic, with a perfectly designed face, and a keen sense of style. I got close to Clara's ear.

- See that guy? - I pointed him. - That's my type.
- Yours and of all gay men. - she provoked me.
- I wanna kiss him.
- Do you?
- Yes.
- Then go there and kiss him.
- I don't know, I am too shy and insecure for that.
- You are shy and insecure in Brazil. Here, you're brave and can get to anyone you want.

I felt challenged, and glad for that feeling. I peered at the boy, who seemed to be alone, and glanced back at Clara. She gave me a look that said *Go!* and I went for it.

I got a little bit high from the drinks so all I remember was approaching him, asking for his name - *Matthew* - and for a kiss. He smiled and we kissed. For hours. From time to time I recognized

Clara passing by us dancing and making fun, always with a drink in her hands. I was feeling happy, and apparently so was she.

Sometime later, less drunk but still cheerful, I noticed I couldn't spot Clara. I asked Matthew to help me find her. We went to all the restrooms, bars, lounges and even outside of the club, and we didn't locate her. I decided to wait for her next to the cloakroom as we had agreed that would be our meeting point in case we got lost. I tried to text her and call her but had no response. Around four in the morning, when the music stopped and the DJ thanked everyone informing that the club would close soon, I started to get really worried. Clara hadn't shown up and I needed to leave. I asked a security guard for help, and she kindly accompanied Matthew and me everywhere in the club, searching for Clara. But we haven't found her. She was not there. The guard guided us to the cloakroom for us to get our belongings back and leave, since the club was closing. To my surprise her coat was there. I asked for it and in the pocket of her jacket was her cell phone, with the missed calls and texts from me. I couldn't understand what was going on.

- Did she leave, without her things, and without telling me? I asked Matthew.

He began to comfort me, as my concern grew stronger. He suggested waiting for her at the deli across the street, and I agreed.

Six o'clock in the morning, the sun was already clear, and still no sign of Clara. My feet were hurting from dancing all night, and a slight hangover made my head also starting to ache. I started gathering hypotheses in my head, but I couldn't come to any conclusions. I was worried about the fact that she didn't have her phone, because there was no other way for me to reach her. I decided to go to her house.

I said goodbye to Matthew, who gave me his phone number and asked me to call later to tell him if everything had turned out well. He had been with me for the past few hours, being extremely generous, and very attentive to the situation. A real gentleman, the kind of guy who would make my head go nuts any time but that. I couldn't think of anything else but finding Clara.

Almost an hour later, with a freshly purchased ice cappuccino at a coffee shop in Queens, and with my hands freezing from holding it, I knocked on the door to the apartment where Clara was living. Her hostess was an eccentric Colombian old lady and the apartment had many ornaments of religious subjects, family photos, and Renaissance paintings. The first and only time I had been there I was introduced to Mrs. Lupita, who looked at me with some curiosity. I think she thought I was romantically interested in Clara, and throughout the time I was there she talked about her youth and the importance of trusting the right people to have a nice life. A somewhat unusual conversation, I thought at the time, for an unpretentious Saturday breakfast while I waited for Clara to get ready to go to the Guggenheim Museum. After pressing the bell and waiting for a few seconds, Mrs. Lupita opened just a little window at the door, where the peephole was supposed to be, and with a suspicious look asked me who I was.

- Good morning, Mrs. Lupita. I'm Vicente, Clara's friend. We were introduced before, when we had breakfast together, remember?

And she continued to stare at me, from the little window, without opening the door.

- Yes, how can I help you? - she asked.

- Clara and I went out last night, and she ended up forgetting her jacket and cell phone with me. I decided to bring them to her, in case she need them. - I omitted from the story the part of her mysterious disappearance because Mrs. Lupita's look was not at all inviting and I thought that if she knew that something like that had happened, I would not seem reliable. Nor would Clara.

Without saying anything, she closed the tiny window. I didn't react, wondering if I should press the bell again or even knock the door. All of a sudden, she opened the door and invited me in. Still serious, she sat me on one of the chairs at the dining table in her all-pink living room.

- Where did you two go last night? - she asked me.

- We went to a bar with some friends from school. - I lied, feeling uncomfortable about making up a story for that lady, and also afraid to contradict myself.

She looked at me thoughtfully, took my both hands in hers, and then smiled.

- You are an angel! God had put you in Clara's path! - she exclaimed in an almost shouted Spanish.

I did not understand what she meant. Not because of the language, but why she had said that.

- Do you know where she is? - she continued, looking me straight in the eye.

I figured I had no choice but to tell her the truth. So, I started slowly.

- Look, Mrs. Lupita, actually Clara and I were together for most of the time, and she ended up forgetting her things with me. I don't know where she is, but...

- She is here. - she interrupted me. - In her bedroom.

I must had looked astonished and relieved at the same time, because she asked me to calm down and offered me a glass of water. After finishing the water, she guided me to the bedroom.

- She's in there, sleeping. She arrived less than an hour ago, wearing a blanket over her clothes. I am worried about her, Vicente. You have the face and the manners of a man who is responsible, so I ask you to help her with that. - she said, opening the door and leading me inside the room. When she closed it, I was left alone with Clara.

The room was dark, with the windows and curtains closed. But it was possible to see Clara lying with one arm stretched out at her side, out of the covers, and wearing a plastic white bracelet. I got closer and saw that it was a hospital ID. I examined the rest of what I could see of her body searching for bruises, but fortunately there were none. Apparently, she was fine. And maybe more comfortable than I was at that moment. Before I could think of anything else, she opened her eyes and whispered.

- Vicente...how crazy is this? Are you alright?

- *I am. Don't know if you are.* - the moment I opened my mouth, I realized I had a censuring tone in my voice. I was scared.

- Dude, I got really bad... Didn't you?

- No. - I answered, almost angry with her. - Clara, I was worried about you. You disappeared from the club. I couldn't find you anywhere.

- Yeah...Where's your date? Matthew, isn't it?

Wasn't she listening to what I was saying?

- Well, he went to his house. And I need to go home too, because it's already morning and I came straight from Splash. So, tell me you're fine.

- I'm fine! - she forced a casual tone. - I think I just need to rest. Tell me about Matthew.

- What happened, Clara? - I ignored her attempt to change the subject.

Realizing that she couldn't make me give up on what had happened, she sat slowly on the bed and started talking.

- Ok. I met a guy, a handsome guy, and I hook up with him. He bought me drinks all night. Maybe too many drinks, I admit. When I started to feel sick, I searched but didn't find you anywhere. I thought you had left the club with Matthew.

I knew for sure I hadn't left the dancefloor or the surroundings, but I let her continue.

- So, I decided to have one more drink with the gorgeous guy, I think his name was Brett. Anyway, next thing I remember is being on a hospital bed, taking glucose in the vein, and feeling very dizzy. - she was faking a dramatic reaction.

- You know you left your belongings at the club, right? How did you managed to get out and check in into a hospital without any IDs?

- I think I passed out at the club and someone drove me to the hospital. At least that's what the doctor told me. And he also said to me that if I was feeling well, I could go home. So, I asked them for a blanket to shelter me from the cold and took the subway.

- And the guy you were with?

- Don't know. - she said, trying to remember some information.

- Clara, this is fucked up. - I said, serious. I was mad at her, not so much for passing out but for trying to make the whole story insignificant. - You know, if it wasn't for me, you would have lost all your belongings, including your passport.

- I know. Oh my God, I'm sorry! - she said, putting her hands over her face, about to cry.

- Ok, calm down. Now you're home, you just need to rest and recover from everything. - I tried to help her, after all.

- Yes, you're right. But what a crazy story, huh? - she almost laughed. - Ok, now tell me about Matthew.

- No, Clara. Now I'm leaving, I need to get rest too. - I was tired and with a slight hangover. - See you in class tomorrow, right?

- Sure! See you tomorrow... - she seemed disappointed.

- Get rest, okay?

She nodded, laying down and closing her eyes.

I left the room and then the apartment, saying goodbye to Mrs. Lupita, who thanked me again before opening the door for me.

Reaching the sidewalk, I felt much colder than I had expected to feel, considering the sunny sky. Actually, the sunlight was starting to bother me more than the cold. Other things were also bothering me at that moment. I was hungry, sleepy and disappointed with Clara. After over an hour riding the subway and still digesting all the events that had started the night before, I arrived home. No sign of Robert in the apartment. *He must be at the church*, I thought. And without showering or brushing my teeth, I lay down on my bed and fell asleep.

CHAPTER IV

Noises coming from the kitchen woke me up, and that was already a pattern. In our initial conversation, Robert had told me that it was not usual for him to use the kitchen, located next to my room, and that he was used to make his meals outside the apartment. This led me to believe that whenever he wanted me to get up and talk to him, he would improvise some dish, intentionally making noise.

I left my bedroom, and saw him at the dining table, eating a slice of pie.

- Good morning, Vicente! - he said, excited. - You have to taste this hazelnut pie. It's from the best bakery in the neighborhood. Come on, sit down.

I accepted his offer and helped myself to a slice. The pie was really delicious. Robert spoke again.

- This afternoon we'll have a church service and I would like you to come with me. You ran away in the last few weeks, but today there is no escape, ok? - he said, with a wide smile. His eyes were bright and his teeth very white.

- Sure, I'll go with you. - I couldn't think of an excuse. I didn't even want to.

I finished the pie and went to get ready. While in the shower, I took time to reflect on how different that activity would be from all the others I had done in the last few weeks. When I arrived in the city, Robert welcomed me not only as a host from whom I was renting a room but as a cordial man always showing a great desire for me to join his company. I had accompanied him to meals around the neighborhood, walks through Fort Tryon Park, had shared some of my daily experiences, mostly from school, and promised to go to one of the church services he usually attended. But, after having more contact with the other parts of the city and sharing experiences with schoolmates, especially with Clara, the frequency with which we did things together had lessened. For some reason I didn't feel quite comfortable with him anymore. Perhaps because I was considering him a figure that referred me to a familiar environment and letting him stay too close could delay my plans to achieve a life different from the one that I had in Brazil. Nevertheless, I put on a very warm outfit and we went out to mass.

A charming ambiance surrounded by stained-glass windows and illuminated by old-fashioned chandeliers, lit even with the day still bright outside, the little chapel gathered about fifty people. Mostly mid-life men and women, everyone was familiar to the prayers and carols that presented pleasant melodies to the ears. From the moment we arrived until the time we left, several friends of Robert introduced themselves to me, praising my host and showing how happy they were that I was there.   I felt very well-received by everybody.

It was inevitable to compare that afternoon with the events of the previous night. They were completely different not to say opposites. In less than twenty-four hours I had been in a gay nightclub accompanied by a new friend, had kissed a handsome man, and had danced to pop music about joy and happiness. At that moment, though, I was in a Christian temple accompanied by an older man, no kisses, and listening to songs about forgiveness and compassion.

The New York that Robert had showed me was not the city I had imagined, but somehow it wasn't bad. I could feel good in that alternate version. Good as I felt at my parents' house, living my old life.

The other New York, the one I had discovered by myself and with Clara's help was the city I had fantasized my whole life. This version had made me feel unprotected at times, almost lost, but always challenged. If I was to choose between the two versions, I wouldn't know which one I would prefer. *Maybe I don't have to choose for now.*

Back home, Robert thanked me for the company, gave me a kiss on the cheek and went to his bedroom. He had never kissed me before, and I found that gesture curious. I had a suspicion about his sexual condition, but although a kiss on the cheek did not make him gay, I felt something different in the air.

The recent events had made me feel homesick and miss talking to my parents. Until that moment, I had called them only twice, once when I arrived to let them know that everything was fine, and again the week before that to catch up on the news. I was avoiding too much contact with them, because it was always a nostalgic experience, and in a way that weakened me, stealing my strength, making me want to return to the familiar coziness and security that I once had.

I decided to call home a third time and talked a few minutes with my parents. Everyone was fine and missing me too. Life went on as usual for them. Talking about my routine to them was something unusual for me because even though we had lived in different houses for years, every time we spoke or got together, I never went into too much detail about certain aspects of my life. In that situation, considering we were really apart, it seemed necessary to talk about trivial things like the weather, my grades at school, about new friendships and the exchange with my host. After hanging up the phone I felt frustrated as always, because it seemed that I wasn't able to express the sensations I was experiencing properly, just with my words. *You would have to be here to understand.*

That night, I cried before sleep. But not out of fear, not out of homesickness not even out of anxiety, as in the past. I cried to release the tension that the whole weekend had made me feel, and because I was already felling different, after only a third of my journey being completed.

Monday, I met Clara on at our first class together at Diplomacy. She had leveled up, so we were in the same classroom.

- Are you feeling better? - I asked, curious to know how she had processed everything that had happened over the weekend.

- I'm feeling brand new. - she answered, kind of making a mockery of my question. And instantly amended - Did you hear about Indian Summer?

- No. What is it? - I didn't want to insist.

- It's a heat wave that arrives here in the US and throughout the northern hemisphere, raising the temperatures for a few days. And it seems to be happening today! - she said, excited.

A warmer weather would be nice, I thought.

At two-thirty, at the end of the class, we went out to lunch. It was already possible to feel the milder weather. I even managed to take off the two coats I was wearing and be left with only a T-shirt. The sun was considerably hot for the first time, and a certain joy arose inside me. I decided to forget about the nightclub episode and not to let a behavior that I thought was wrong jeopardize the bond of strong friendship that I had achieved with Clara. *After all, nobody's perfect, right?*

A Mc Donald's meal later, I insisted that we took a walk down Fifth Avenue, which looked different that day, with the bright sunlight and the reflected blue sky on the windows of major branded stores. It might have been my perception, but people on the streets seemed happier than they had been in the past weeks, and that affected me too. We spent the whole afternoon strolling, shopping, and we even had ice cream, something Clara had refused to do with before because of the cold weather. We visited toy stores and went to an Apple Store, where I bought a new notebook. Then, as we were looking for a place to sit and rest at Rockefeller Center, a large church across the street caught my attention, The St. Patrick's Cathedral.

- Wanna come in? - I invited Clara.

- In a church?

- Yes, we can sit inside.

- Alright! I can take the opportunity and pray for my family. - agreed, Clara. I found the praying interesting.

The cathedral had an imposing interior, all carved in a stone that appeared to be marble, and large sculptures of sacred-themed images. Unlike the temple I had been to the night before, everything there looked grand and even inspiring luxury. We sat in one of the first rows and took a moment contemplating the altar wrapped in large and tall stone pillars. It was impossible not to be impressed by the beauty of that place, and the fact that it was a church did not diminish its architectural importance. On the contrary, the construction seemed to have been made to exalt divine perfection. Clara got down on her knees using the bench's support, apparently to pray. I sat there, thinking about positive things.

Whenever I went to churches, which was not very frequently, I used to pray but in Portuguese. I found that there my prayers would not make sense, as I didn't know their English version. Thus, using the language that I was there to improve, I asked for my path to be revealed to me, and for me to be able to discern it and follow it. Then I started to think about everything that had happened to me since I had arrived in the city, about all the questions still unanswered, and some certainties that were beginning to point out in my mind. I thought about how faith, separate from religion, was fundamental and was helping me to maintain optimism and calm in times of doubt. And I thought about how Clara had surprised me by showing a religious side, previously hidden. That made me complacent about her previous behavior. She was also going through a moment of change and was searching for answers, just like me, and one or two missteps could be part of that journey.

It was unexpected how, for a moment, I felt just as comfortable there as at the temple visited with Robert the previous day. I stayed there with Clara for a few more minutes. Then we got up, lighted two of the many candles in a row near the altar and left.

Leaving the cathedral and stepping into the sidewalk was an immediate contrast for me. The spirituality I had experienced minutes before seemed not to fit the city. I remembered Robert's negative reaction towards New York, in one of our first talks, and how that had startled me. I remembered the comfort I felt at the apartment and at the small church. Perhaps he didn't know how to fit a religious life into the chaos of a metropolis. But that cathedral seemed to succeed on the task. Then I thought about all the learning I had gained making new friends, visiting new places and discovering new tastes in different areas of Manhattan. I was constantly leaving my comfort zone, without giving away my core values. To me that was evolution. *Had Robert tried to take chances like that?*

Back on Fifth Avenue, we led to Central Park. We spent the whole afternoon walking the winding roads of the park, until the night fell. Tired of the hot and busy day, each of us went back home.

Robert was waiting for me to have our usual night chat, and I told him about the visit to St. Patrick's.

- Did you go there to ask for forgiveness?

- What do you mean? - I was surprised by the question.

- Have you had a non-standard behavior? - he asked, with a steady look, which made me uncomfortable.

- I don't think so...

- Are you sure? - he continued to stare at me.

- Actually, I wanted to see the difference between a church here in the neighborhood and a church Midtown...

- I'm messing with you! - he said, laughing. - Have a good night. - and still laughing, went to his bedroom.

I just managed to laugh nervously, as I didn't understand the intent of that joke. I thought that, as we had gone to the chapel the day before, my visit to the cathedral could be a good subject to talk to him. But he seemed to me not only sarcastic but bizarre in general. Even his laugh sounded different, maybe even cruel. I went to sleep thoughtful again, with Robert as a puzzle in my mind.

The following days were gifted with a pleasant temperature, and Clara and I took the opportunity to enjoy activities like cycling on the streets Downtown, walking through Highline Park, strolling along the Ninth and Tenth Avenues in search of a different cafe, discovering good drinks and snacks in the Meatpacking District, venturing out on long trails through Central Park, and having a lot of ice cream. The suggested activities from school no longer seemed to matter to Clara, and I wasn't too keen to have other colleagues around, especially the Brazilian ones who insisted on using our native language to communicate. And then one morning broke out very clear and windy. The cold had returned, and Halloween had arrived.

Diplomacy had prepared a celebration for the date, and all students were invited to go to class in costumes. The previous day Clara and I had spent the whole afternoon looking for different and funny costumes and ended up like Michael Jackson and Hello Kitty. Characters from movies and comic books, music personalities and heroes from different cultures circulated through the school corridors, making that day different from the usual. Everyone was very relaxed and excited for a get-together that the school would do after the classes, at the hall next to the reception. Typical food such as pumpkin pies and sweets imitating spiders and witches' brooms were waiting for students at a large table, available to anyone who would want to have lunch there. Clara and I agreed to eat just a little and avoid the crowd of students that was starting to show up. Before we left, Clara asked me to accompany her to the computer lab. After forty minutes checking her e-mails while I was standing next to her, not interested in checking mine, I got tired of waiting.

- Let's go have lunch, Clara. - I called her. I was also hungry, despite having tasted a couple of candies from the Halloween table.

- Come on, just one more minute.

I noticed that she was talking to someone, exchanging messages on the computer.

- Is that your new lover? - I teased her, seeing a picture of a boy on the screen.

- No, he's just a friend. - she said shutting down the computer, taking her bag and standing up. - Ok, let's go.

We made our way to Austin's Café on Seventh Avenue. Clara had already met some men in recent weeks, most of them foreigners, and she had always shared her stories with me. None of them had won more than one night with her and she bragged that she was breaking hearts. I had to give her credit as I used to follow the continuous messages sent to her cell phone after the dates, when they begged for a second round. I hadn't been with anyone since Matthew, but I was willing to have another experience like that soon. After lunch, I followed Clara to her house, so she could hand over the rent to Mrs. Lupita. When Clara went to the bathroom, the lady immediately pulled me into the kitchen.

- Vicente, I'm worried about Clara. - she said, hurriedly.

- Why is that? - I asked.

- See, she has brought different men here, and they all had slept with her. I have no problem with that, but she is getting different.

- What do you mean by different, Mrs. Lupita? - I found it a little funny, like she was sounding like her mother and not like a hostess.

- I don't know how to explain. But I think she is less affectionate with me. She barely talks when she arrives, and she leaves the house without warning me. She used to be more caring.

I didn't know how to politely say to her that Clara was not her daughter, just a girl renting a room in her apartment. Maybe Mrs. Lupita was mixing things.

- Keep an eye on her, please. - she asked me.

- Sure, no problem. - I agreed, trying to reassure her, but thinking that she was probably overreacting, although I was also noticing a change at Clara's behavior. I understood Mrs. Lupita's concern since Clara was inside her home, and the lady seemed very conventional about social conducts. But although Clara seemed to be a little loopy sometimes, I knew she was a good girl. At least I believed that. Despite everything, I decided to pay more attention to the way she was acting.

Clara returned to the living room, and I joined her. We watched the *Friends* marathon that was broadcast on the television, dubbed in Spanish, while eating popcorn for the rest of the afternoon. At six o'clock, we went out to see the traditional Greenwich Village Halloween parade.

We had been to the Village before, but that night the neighborhood was exceptionally noteworthy. A real crowd gathered on the streets, most wearing spooky costumes, and fireworks bursting in the sky from time to time. On the main avenue the parade was starting. Allegory-rich cars, despite not equal to the artistic monuments that are usually seen at the Rio de Janeiro carnival, were setting the vibe of the party, exploring black, purple and orange elements throughout its extent. Ghosts were floating above whoever was closest to the sidewalk, which was not our case, mine and Clara's, because we were a little further away, near a bar's entrance. Ghastly figures, witches, monsters and other characters from the horror universe passed one by one on top of the cars, or below on the street, dancing and trying to scare the excited spectators. That whole scenario reminded me of a folklore festival that used to be set in the city where I was born and grew up, when people dressed in a fantasy depicting an ox and paraded down the street of my grandmother's house, scaring people. My grandmother was afraid of these figures, but in the end we all laughed, as the real intention was to have fun. At that moment, the purpose was also to have fun, but I was not feeling so happy. Clara was not talkative and sympathetic as usual, and that was enough for me to remember my conversation with Mrs. Lupita.

Suddenly, three visibly drunk boys came out of the bar. They were speaking loudly, bumping against each other on purpose and laughing. In New York it was forbidden to drink alcohol outside establishments, and in my opinion the three of them had drunk everything they could inside and were ready to party outside. One of them looked in our direction and shouted:

- Clarita! There you are!

- Juan? - responded Clara, excited.

Before I could tell, the two were hugging and calling the other two guys to join them.

- Vicente, this is Juan - Clara turned to me - and these are Luiz and Diego. - she continued.

I greeted them from a distance. It was obvious that Clara knew the three boys, but I had never seen them before. On a second look, I could actually recognize one of them from the school's computer screen when Clara was checking her e-mails earlier. I waited for her to continue with the introductions, hoping to find out where they had met. But instead, she skipped that part and continued:

- We agreed to meet here at the parade, to go to a party. - she told me. And turned to them - Right, guys?

The three guys nodded. Juan said something to Clara in a Spanish that I couldn't understand, full of slangs, reached out to her, and discreetly handed her something. I couldn't see what it was because the action was fast, and the object was small enough to fit in the palm of a closed hand. Clara took the object from Juan's hand and put it in her coat pocket, in a quick movement. I found that suspicious but said nothing. Then, Juan signaled the two friends to walk and moved on. Clara and I followed the three, two steps behind.

- Where's this party? - I asked her.

- I don't know, but it'll be so much fun! - she said without looking at me.

- I didn't know we were going to a party. I thought we would just check the parade and then decide what to do together, me and you.

- Oh, Vicente, I forgot to tell you. My bad. - she was still looking ahead.

- Okay, but I 'm not sure about this party. I probably don't know anyone there and ...

- Me neither! I only know Juan. But the intention is precisely this, to make new friends.

- I don't know, Clara ...

She stopped and looked at me.

- Come on, Vicente! You have to go with me, you can't leave me alone. - she raised her voice.

- I don't wanna leave you alone. But you arranged this without telling me. I thought we would do another kind of activity. And besides, I didn't like these guys... - I kept my voice down so they wouldn't hear me.

- Why not? - she kept her voice loud.

- I don't know, they're already drunk and speaking nonsense... And what did Juan give you?

- It's nothing, just a little something to enjoy the party.

- Drugs, Clara?

- Oh man, don't be so grumpy! - she walked again. I followed her.

- Aren't you afraid of being sick the same way as you were that night at Splash? - the idea crossed my mind in a disturbing way.

- Of course not! That was an exception. It's not gonna happen again. - she seemed sure about that. - Come on, Vicente! Let's go! - she started walking faster to reach the boys.

I was not happy about that mysterious party, about our companionships, or about the drug hidden in Clara's pocket. I had clear in my head that that party meant trouble, and that we shouldn't go. But apparently, she wasn't listening to me.

The three guys were practically running, and so did we.

- I don't know, Clara. Where do you know Juan from?

- A friend introduced us.

- What friend?

- A friend you don't know.

She was obviously hiding things from me. I wouldn't go to that party.

- I think we better go get something to eat... - I tried to change her mind one last time.

- No! - she shouted at me. - Are you trying to ruin my night, Vicente? Is that it? - she stopped at an intersection on the street.

I was taken aback. Clara had never raised her voice to me, much less had looked self-centered as she did at that moment. I remembered once more about Mrs. Lupita's request for me.

- Clara, let's say goodbye to them and go elsewhere. - I insisted firmly.

- I'm going to the party! -she continued shouting. - If you don't wanna go with me, be a man and say it.

Clara looked at me in a different light, waiting for me to say something.

- Well, I don't wanna go to this stupid party. - I said, serious.

Her face was taken by an angry expression.

- Ok, whatever. - she turned and walked away towards Juan and the two boys.

- Clara! - I shouted.

She didn't look back.

I returned home saddened by what had happened, and worried about what might. *Was Clara being selfish? Or was I being too rigid?*

CHAPTER V

Saturday dawned brightly through the curtains of my room, and I decided to enjoy the weekend by myself. I woke up, took a long shower, put on one of my new recently bought outfits and my backpack, and took the subway. All the way Downtown I wondered what to do, and breakfast at Stumptown on 29th Street seemed like a good idea. That region was already my new favorite neighborhood, where I had spent most of my days, and in a way, it was quite a safe space for me.

Sitting in one of the few vacant spots I could find, with my Frappuccino on the table, I opened my notebook and checked in a social network website where I was registered for some time, G-Radar. My longtime friends from Brazil and I were used to access those kinds of websites to meet new people, and to set dates with other men. I hadn't checked my messages since I left Brazil, and to my surprise some guys had tried to make contact since then. Meeting people in New York was my new goal, and the main one that weekend, so I altered my location to Manhattan, and hoped my English would help with future conversations.

Five minutes later, while reading a Time Out Magazine, a few guys started to chat with me through G-Radar. I spent the rest of the morning learning new slang, discovering the trendy places to go for gays in my age group and feeling more sociable and fit-in than ever in that metropolis. At least, virtually.

I arranged to meet one of the guys I talked to, for lunch nearby, in Chelsea. As I didn't know where the restaurant was, we agreed to find each other in front of the building. When I arrived, I saw a tall man, very well dressed, with brown straight hair, and a wide smile standing in front of the door.

- Vicente? - he asked, taking off his sunglasses.

- Yes. Raul, right?

- Yes, that's me! Shall we go inside?

Raul was my age, but unlike his photo on the website he looked older in person. The restaurant was one of the most beautiful I had visited since I arrived in the city, and I felt a little out of place, as I had a backpack that didn't quite fit with the classy vibe of the ambiance. I hadn't expected the meeting to be in such a formal environment. We sat down and were immediately attended by a friendly waiter who brought us still water and a basket of bread and pâtés.

- I gotta tell you, you're even more gorgeous in person. - said Raul.

- Thanks. - I wanted to say the same to him, but I was feeling shy.

- What brings you to New York, Vicente?

- Well, it's a long story.

And it was indeed. Over the course of nearly one hour, I tried to summarize what had driven me to travel abroad, and much of what had happened so far, without going into too much personal detail. Raul seemed interested.

- Now tell me *your* story. - I asked.

And then he spent the next hour or so talking about how he had left Turkey and decided to study Fashion in New York, going up against his father because of it. He was living alone, and attending the last year of study, preparing his collection for the final project in college. We had already talked about the same subjects in our brief website-chat earlier, but in person other matters came up, and when we realized, two hours had passed, and in the middle of a very tasty lunch we had laughed a lot and spent a great time together. Raul then invited me to his apartment.

- I have a beautiful view, you'll like it.

- Ok, I'll accept the invitation. But only because of the sight, ok? - I joked. He smiled.

It was not just the view that was appealing in the apartment. Upon entering, I instantly realized that the decor was fantastic, as if it came out of a famous interior design magazine. I accepted a glass of wine and we went to the sofa. I kept worried about balancing that glass, afraid to dye the white and soft sofa with the red and strong cabernet, while Raul was hugging and kissing me. I didn't know much about wines, and didn't like red ones very much, but that one really pleased me.

- Let's go to the bedroom. - he said, very polite, even though he seemed more uninhibited than me.

- Are you sure? - I asked him, wanting to go but wondering if I was sure of that.

- Yes, very sure. - he confirmed.

I let myself be carried away by the moment and the effect of the wine, and we end up having sex. All along Raul was loving and that made me feel good. I was experiencing something new. It was the first time I was sleeping with anyone since I had arrived in the United States, but I didn't realize it until we were done. After taking a quick shower, Raul lent me a towel and I washed myself too. I put on my clothes and was prepared to leave.

- Are you leaving? Already? - he made a sad face, hugging me tight.

- Yes, I got a few errands to run today. - I said the first thing that came into my mind. Part of me was enjoying being there, but another part was forcing myself to go. Raul had been great until that moment but suddenly Lucas came to my mind and the whole situation struck me as odd. I knew I needed to move on and going out with other men was part of that, maybe even an essential part of it, in order to forget about the past. But I felt I needed to take it easy.

- Can I call you later? - he asked me.

- Of course. - I replied naturally, hoping he wouldn't.

From the sidewalk outside the building I looked up and saw him in the huge window of his apartment, looking back at me. I felt awkward. The whole scenario looked like a farewell scene from a movie, involving two boyfriends who would miss each other. His face was showing exactly that expression, of someone who had already started counting the seconds for the next meeting. And that scared me a little. I wasn't looking for love, I was actually running away from it, trying to turn it into something else. And Raul seemed to be willing to tie himself to someone as soon as possible. I didn't want to play with his feelings. So, I didn't respond to the text message he sent me hours later. Or to his call, that same night.

Before going to bed, as I thought about what had happened, I realized that I had never managed to be so relaxed about a good date like I was being. Usually, when I had a positive outcome from a date, I used to plan the next steps right after. This had led me to complicated circumstances in recent years, and perhaps at that moment a little evolution could be noticed in me. And there was one person I wanted to tell about it. I just didn't know if our relationship was still the same.

I met Clara on Monday, in the classroom. I had secretly hoped that she would be absent, so I wouldn't have to confront my dilemma between running away from her, as I still felt hurt by our argue, or running to her and tell about my weekend. This confusion bothered me, but at the same time avoided a disappointment. The class went on typically, except for the palpable silence between us all morning. As we had no activities in the afternoon that day, we were released early for lunch. When everyone started to leave the room, Clara looked at me for the first time that day and smiled. I wanted to seem indifferent, but I only managed to smile back. I couldn't deny that we had built a beautiful friendship during the first month of our new lives, and we had been accomplices in several experiences so far. I approached her, making conversation.

- How was your weekend?

- Well, same as always. You know, parties, lovers, Mrs. Lupita being a pain in the ass...

It was not the first time that Clara was referring to Mrs. Lupita like that, but before it had sounded funny, as if she was amusingly teasing her hostess. That day her speech was different, as if scorning everything and everyone. And there was also something unusual in her features. Her eyes seemed tired, as if she hadn't slept well.

-   Parties? - I asked, wanting to know more.

-   Yep. I've met some very cool people. - she said with a cold voice, as if trying to provoke me. - Hey, are we gonna talk forever or can we have lunch? I'm starving.

The mood between us was still weird.

We ate at a Chinese self-service restaurant close to the school, before entering Forever 21 in Times Square so that Clara could choose a dress for her evening date.

- What do you think of this one? - she showed me a black short dress with very thin straps and a revealing neckline. She looked uncomfortable in the dress.

- It's beautiful. But I never saw you in that kind of outfit, Clara... - I was surprised by the forced attempt to appear sensual. She was very charming, but not the kind of girl who used to wear short or tight pieces to be noticed. Her clothes were usually less revealing and more comfortable and stylish.

- That's my new style. - she said firmly. And then flashed a broad smile.

She kept looking through a world of garments, asking for my opinion but not always taking my notes in consideration. In the end, she ended up telling me about some of the parties she had gone to on Saturday, about guys she had met, and about conducts that I considered too dangerous, like drinking outdoors and going out with new friends who, by her description, were clearly drug dealers. It all seemed like a lot of fun for Clara, but although her contagious laughter diminished that strangeness between us, I noticed a difference in the way she was facing her new life. I told her about my date with

Raul and she highlighted the fact that it had been my first time since Lucas and that that was an evolution for me, just as I expected her reaction to be. From the outside, our relationship had returned to normal, but Clara was no longer the same person for me. Before, I considered her to be a feminine version of me, in appropriate proportions, and that was why it had made sense that we spent time together, with similar goals towards the city and the future. At that moment, she looked like a version of me who had succumbed to dazzles and hopelessness. An even greater contrast compared to Robert, the other reference I had. Not long ago, I had wondered on how there were two sides of the city that I was experiencing. A more spiritual, safe, familiar one with Robert, and a more real, free and challenging one with Clara. I hadn't thought it was required of me to choose between the two sides, as they were opposite but not conflicting. However, little by little Robert's unstable behavior was no longer making me comfortable, and Clara's company was starting to seem less and less attractive, because it was following a path that didn't appeal to me. I wanted challenges and independence, but I also wanted to learn to create my own limits within them. And apparently neither Robert nor Clara were being able to help me with that.

It was time for me to start standing on my own two feet on the Big Apple and take a third path. My own.

CHAPTER VI

G-Radar chats had become my great distraction during my free time, especially when at home on weeknights. In the previous days, I had spent time walking around Manhattan and visiting neighborhoods like East Village and West Village and their charming little cafes and bookstores, visiting museums in search of inspiration for future photographic works, and enjoying a more classic part of the island in the Upper East Side. In addition, I had toured different stores from famous brands to thrift ones, in search of new garments that would translate my new and more independent New Yorker style, and that would also keep me warm. My new iPod had become my frequent companion, coloring my rides with songs distinct from the ones I used to hear, making me feel different and more courageous.

Despite starting to go out more by myself, I was still the companion for Clara on some of our customary hobbies such as meals at our favorite restaurants and occasional shopping adventures. I couldn't totally avoid her, and actually I didn't want to. Part of me had created a lot of consideration for her, a feeling similar to that of a sibling, and kind of a need to protect her. But eventually, during our conversations, she would start consuming me with complaints about her hostess, her affective problems with the many men with whom she had contact, and the growing homesickness. I was constantly trying to be supportive and help her with positive speeches, but eventually started to think that the case was more serious and that she was probably dealing into depression, even though she wasn't aware of it. As a result, cynicism had also become her frequent companion.

One afternoon, during a stop at a Starbucks, after leaving a home decor store, Clara excused herself and went out for a smoke. She had acquired this habit a few weeks earlier, and at first it didn't bother me. But at that stage, I was often having to choose between being left alone but breathing clean air inside places or follow her outside and inhale her smoke.

- Clara, before you leave, can I ask you something? - I had to talk to her about that.

- Wow, what a ceremony! Ask me.

- I don't know how else to ask that, so... Don't you think you might be depressed?

- Why do you say that? - she asked, startled.

- Because I'm feeling you more tired than usual, even a little sad. I know you've been missing home, but I don't think that's all it is. - I tried to be thoughtful but had to be honest with her. - Besides, you told me you've been having trouble sleeping.

- Well, I am really tired, but I think it's the cold. Don't you feel the same way?

- A little bit, I guess. But I think I have been more concerned about my health than you with yours. - *Was I being too incisive?*

- Look, Vicente, I'm great, ok? You're exaggerating, as always. - she said, standing up. - I'll be right back. - and went out to smoke.

Outside she lit a cigarette and started dialing on her cell phone. That was another behavior she had acquired: spending hours, literally hours, on the phone. About that, there was nothing I could do unless stay by her side waiting for the call to end and hoping for her to realize she was wasting time and not living the moment. Ending the conversation and the cigarette, she came back in again and sat down, silent and frowning.

- Problems? - I asked, half worried, half provoking her.

- No. - she was concise.

- Was the cigarette bad? - I then tried to joke, to get a smile from her. It didn't work.

I saw that a tear was running down her face.

- Clara, what happened? Bad news over the phone? - I was really worried.

- No, it has nothing to do with it.

- What it is, then?

- I don't know.

- How come you don't know?

- Vicente, do you think the cigarette is hurting me? - she asked me in a sweet voice.

- I'm sure it's bad for your health, if that's what you're asking me. - it was my chance to make her realize the importance of taking better care of her health, and also avoid having to inhale more smoke.

- But you see, I've smoked other times, and it had never hurt me.
Damn, she was stubborn.

- Ok. Then why are you crying? - I asked her.

Silence and more tears. I moved to the chair beside her and hugged her. We stayed like that for some time. I decided not to push on that matter anymore, since she was fragile.

- Well, let's go, I have to meet Tom tonight and I can't have a swollen face. - she said, suddenly standing up and grabbing her bag.

Tom was one of the guys she was seeing that week, friend of a friend I didn't know.

- Don't you think it's better to do something more relaxed today? You really don't look well to me. How about a movie with lots of popcorn? - I tried to cheer her up.

- Are you crazy? I cannot cancel this date. - she seemed outraged.

- Why not? Reschedule for another day.

- No! And come on, I lost track of time. - she was standing while I was still seated.

- I'll stay here a little longer, Clara. - I intently crossed my arms on the table to show her I was not moving. I was not on the mood to repeat the Halloween argue.

- You're really not following me? - she sounded furious.

- Follow you? Sorry, but no. - I was losing my temper but managed to stay calm. - Honestly, I'll take my time to... - and before I could tell her anything, she interrupted me.

- Yep, take your time to master the art of being boring! Wow, Vicente, you've been almost unbearable lately. - she spoke in anger and walked towards the door.

I almost didn't believe what I heard. And I didn't have time to reply, because when I realized she was out of the cafe. Clara's behavior was definitely changed, and there was no longer any doubt that she was being self-centered. And that that was affecting our friendship. I had probably been overcritical about her, but most of the time she was lacking consideration towards me. Avoiding her would be unfortunately necessary and also easier now, as I had leveled up at school, leaving her behind. *Maybe she needs to find her own path by herself too.*

I went home early and had dinner with Robert. I wasn't able to get away from his invitation, like other times. Every interaction with him was making me more certain about my opinion that he was a confusing and extremely needy being, with stories of pleasant beginnings and dubious endings. Sometimes I pretended to care about the conversation so that he could think I was a good listener but, in the end, I always felt bad about it, thinking I could actually learn more from him if he was more pleasant, and less sarcastic about every matter. Maybe we didn't have things in common after all, and that was fine with me. Although he constantly insisted on having a stronger bond, I decided that it wasn't crucial for me to be the perfect guest and that it was okay not to have a close relationship with him.

I spent the rest of the night chatting through G-Radar and setting dates. I needed new friends.

- I can't believe you've never been to Rio! - said Louis, surprised.

- Never... - I admitted, pretending to be ashamed.

Louis was an attractive, red-haired and thin North American who had been raised in Miami and was living in New York, due to his work. He had already traveled, also on business, to other countries including Brazil. And I couldn't believe how little I knew about my own country as I talked to him.

- You should spend some time in Florianopolis. The city has beautiful beaches. And beautiful landscapes. And beautiful guys.

- Oh yes, I know Floripa. And I agree with you. But New York also has a beautiful view. - I joked, looking at him.

- Mine, today, is the best in town.

I must have blushed because he smiled very seductively at me.

We were sitting on a bench near the Brooklyn Museum, facing each other, and the afternoon started to give way to the night, lowing the temperature and increasing my feeling of cold. Louis invited me to his apartment, in a gorgeous building nearby, and I accepted.

He lived with a colleague, who was out the moment we arrived. He sat me down on the couch and went into the kitchen to prepare chocolate chip cookies for us to eat while watching a comedy movie on cable. The movie wasn't so funny, but it didn't matter, because in less than half an hour we were moving our kissing from the couch to the bed. And the kisses became stronger caresses, which turned into hugs, and when I realized our clothes were on the floor and we were having sex. This time I was more aware, during the act, of what I was doing. Despite that one being another extremely affectionate guy, besides being handsome and friendly, I was not able to feel anything but physical pleasure. It felt good, it was easy, but it wasn't worth it. And although the sex had been satisfying, I just wanted to go home. And so, I did.

Later, checking my e-mails, something I had avoided doing too much in order to keep the focus on my new life, I saw at a glance a message from Lucas. *Hi! How are things? Miss you.* - he had written. The vague words made it clear how far he was from my life. So distant, that I felt in my core I was beginning to overcome the sadness regarding his friendship request. I had never believed in soul mates. I had always thought that there were some people for each person, depending on the circumstances, after all the world is very large and extremely populated. But at that moment, I was not interested in meeting any of these possible people. I just wanted to meet new guys, maybe new friends. If not possible, at least have new stories, meet new cultures and have a new lifestyle.

I was halfway through my journey, a month and a half in town and still a month and a half from my departure. A few classmates started to say goodbye to New York that week and that would become common in the following months. I went out with some colleagues from Diplomacy to have lunch and say goodbye to Tanaka, who was returning to Japan. We hadn't stayed close friends through his stay, but I had enjoyed his company in the few times we went out together, so I made it a point to be present at his farewell.

Tanaka arrived at the Hard Rock Café in Times Square after everyone has, with an emotional look although smiling. During the meal, I had a chance to ask him what he was taking back home as an experience for his life.

- You know, Vicente, I stayed in the city for just over a month, but it has changed my life. Seeing how things happen here made me more willing to face some challenges there, in my small city in Japan. - he said, in a clearly farewell speech.

- That's great! I'm happy for you. - I said, genuinely glad for him. It was that kind of lesson that I wanted to take with me when I return to Brazil, but I still didn't feel that I had achieved half of what I needed.

Clara was also present, but since she didn't know most of the people there, she was silent almost the entire time, talking exclusively to me now and then. After a delicious dessert and a Happy Birthday sung by the waiters, we offered our best wishes to Tanaka. When we were leaving the restaurant, Clara asked me to escort her to a friend's home in Harlem.

- What's there for us, Clara? - I asked, not very excited by the idea.

- Joe's apartment. He is Tom's friend, remember Tom? - I nodded, although I had never seen the guy in person, only heard about him through her stories. - He's renting a room, and I'm interested in it. - continued.

- But you already rent a room, from Mrs. Lupita. - I said the obvious, realizing her intentions.

- Yep, but that old woman is driving me crazy! - she said in a rude tone. - I need to move out as soon as possible! You don't have space for me in your bedroom, do you?

- No, and my host would never let us both occupy the same room. - I said, immediately refusing a possible request from Clara for us to live together. The last thing I needed at that moment was to share my space with someone, much less with her. - Let's go to Harlem, then. - I hurried my step towards the subway, to end the conversation.

Sometime later, after missing the street a few times, we arrived at Joe's apartment. The place was nice, ground floor, airy and new. But I didn't have the same good impression about the people we met there. Six young students living together, dividing their space among four bedrooms, and having the common areas stuffed by everyone's belongings and obviously needing a cleaning. After we got to know the whole apartment, Joe took us to the porch and lit a marijuana cigarette. Without ceremony, he simply handed it over to Clara, who acted as if that was customary. She smoked it and passed it on to a girl, who lived there, and who after offered it to me. I refused it and went out to the restroom, an excuse for not having to inhale another type of smoke from Clara. I sensed she was somehow more intimate with those people than she was with me, and also seemed happier to be in their company. Also, it became clear to me that she hadn't quit smoking, if worse she was doing it even more.

- What did you think about the apartment? - Clara asked me on the subway on our way home.

- Clara, the apartment is very nice. But you would have to share your bedroom, something that you don't have to do in our current apartment. - I wanted to keep myself from telling her that I didn't like the whole idea of moving out.

- Yeah, I know, you're probably right about that. - She seemed to consider my opinion. -You didn't like Joe, did you? Are you jealous?

- Jealous? - *What was she talking about?* - I'm worried about you, that's what it is!

- Vicente, I know how to take care of myself! I already told you that.

I don't think so, I thought to myself.

- But if you wanna know, I decided I won't move anyway. - she continued. - Too many people together end up in problem. I'll see how much longer I can take the old Lupita. - she said, with a tone of disdain when pronouncing the lady's name.

- Clara, don't talk about her like that.

- Ok, now you're gonna say you love your host? Didn't you tell me that you always run away from his invitations?

- Yes, I do. But that's simply because of my goals here in New York.

- Oh yeah, your goals. Have you reached any of them so far? - she asked me, in a defiant tone and already sounding unpleasant, as in every end of conversation we were having in weeks.

- Yes. I've already improved my English, I've met new and nice people, I'm forgetting about Lucas, and I feel much less dependent on things and people. - I responded, feeling challenged.

- Congratulations! - she said, looking happy, changing her expression suddenly, as if she were playing a mysterious game with the purpose of making me angry and then showing some sympathy. A very confusing game. - Let's celebrate then! Let's go to Splash! - she sounded very excited.

- Do you wanna go again to the club where you passed out the last time? - I asked, wishing she would say yes, because I was in the mood to dance, after all.

- Yes! But without the fainting part. - she laughed. I hated it when she would make a joke and laugh, because that way she was able to win me back for a few seconds, causing all the armor I had created to dismantle. And the hope that her behavior could change allowing her to be the Clara that I knew, the Clara from before, was reborn in me.

That late afternoon, we both went shopping for a special look for the occasion.

I had arranged a date with a French man who lived in New York that night, so I called him to meet at Splash. Clara loved the idea.

We met Pierre at the entrance of the club, and the three of us got in together. As usual, the DJ took great care in the music selection, the lights made the dancefloor look like a big blue and green aquarium calling everyone to dance, and the bar was full of people enjoying their drinks. Pierre was not as friendly as Raul or Louis, limiting himself to dance quietly and eventually kiss me. The lack of conversation left me a little dismayed, and when he said he needed to leave, after two hours, I didn't care too much. We said goodbye and I went to look for Clara. I found her wrapped in kisses and hugs with a boy much taller than her, but who appeared to be much younger, possibly a minor. I approached them, poked her in the back, and told her that Pierre was gone.

- Do you wanna leave too? - she asked me, with an expression of who was not enjoying the company.

- If you want to... - I said, giving her the cue to escape from the boy.

- Let's go, then! - she said hurriedly, turning to the boy, saying something I could not hear, and following me to the cloakroom.

Fifteen minutes later, in an Anthora on Seventh Avenue and over a cup of coffee, I told her about the lack of chemistry between Pierre and me.

- Maybe you don't want just one night of sex, Vicente.

- Well, I'm not looking for a boyfriend. But that doesn't mean I can't have the conversation part, to know each other a little bit. I like that part. Is that too much to ask?

- No, of course not. But talking too much is a risk, you know? You can grow more intimacy, and then one thing can lead to another, and when you realize, you are in love.

- No way! - I laughed, to show her how much I disagreed about that theory, but internally agreeing a little bit with it.

- What do you want, after all? - she questioned me.

- I want to meet new people and have a good time. No expectations.

- I'm doing exactly this. - she said, taking a sip of coffee.

She was right. I just didn't agree with the way she was doing it. I thought she was better than that.

- And have you forgotten about your old boyfriend? What's his name again? - I asked.

- Esteban. - she answered. - I haven't completely forgotten about him yet, but I still have a few months here to achieve that. *You* have to hurry to forget about Lucas.

Clara would stay in New York for six months, double the time I would stay in the city.

- I'm not here exclusively for that. - I said - I'm meeting other guys because I want to have new experiences. Forgetting about Lucas should be a consequence of that.

- Oh yeah, sure! You've been going out with one guy after another, hoping to find your next boyfriend, Vicente! - she said, using a tone I didn't like.

- I disagree, Clara. And it hasn't been one guy after another. - I said, starting to get uncomfortable with that conversation. - You have been following me closely, and you know that I have been selective about the guys I've been dating...

- Are you? - she interrupted me, crossing her arms on her chest level. - Then why did you kiss Pierre, if there was no chemistry between you two?

- I don't know, I felt like it.

She kept looking at me, hoping for a better explanation. I didn't have it.

- And you, why did you kiss that minor? - I changed the focus to her.

- First of all, he was not a minor. And I kissed him because I want and desperately need to forget Esteban. The difference is that I admit that.

Clara was showing herself different in many ways, but her commitment to the truth was still evident as always. And hearing that I wasn't admitting something important made me wonder if I was lying to myself. I hadn't thought too much about my behavior in a few weeks, I was just living my life. In my head, it was clear that the trip had been decided before Lucas requested for us to be just friends, and I didn't consider this episode as one of the main reasons. Not until I arrived in the city. The purpose of spending a hundred days in New York came from the need to learn how to live alone, to do things on my own, to grow as a person, and to be able to set goals for the future, regardless of people or places. I was managing to do that, and I started to feel that forgetting Lucas was also possible. Clara's remark about him was not entirely out of context, but perhaps my behavior had made her think that way. I still talked about him from time to time, as he was my last relationship reference. And I always tended to accept her opinions about love and life, as if everything I had ever lived had not made me learn a little about these subjects as well. I needed to leave my previous references behind, and that directly implied stop talking about past relationships.

- Okay, Clara. I admit that forgetting Lucas is among my goals. But I haven't been doing it *desperately*, as you say you are.

- But if you don't really try, you won't be able to. - she insisted.

- I'm trying, but I have other more important goals to achieve too. - I needed to defend my point of view.

- Well, you're an adult and you know what you do. - she took another sip of her coffee, in a sign that that conversation was over.

- Yes, you and I are adults. Unlike that boy you kissed. - I wanted to provoke her, for fun.

- He was eighteen, Vicente! Don't fuck with me, come on. - she said, laughing.

Clara knew me well, and we were very similar in many ways. Keep her away could make me miss an opportunity for growth. But at that point our relationship was working because we were seeing each other less than before. She was like a mirror that reflected my weaknesses and doubts about the past and the future, and to be constantly in front of it wasn't being entirely healthy for me.

That morning I accompanied her to Queens, and decided to sleep there, after all the subway was under maintenance and it would take hours for me to get home.

CHAPTER VII

My birthday was approaching, and it would be my first time spending the date away from my family and friends, so I needed to find a proper way to celebrate it. With the help of Clara and using the internet, I had chosen to have dinner at Acqua, a restaurant on the Upper West Side, followed by cocktails and music at G-Lounge, a bar in the West Village. I invited some colleagues from Diplomacy to meet us on Saturday and be part of the celebration.

During the previous week, I had resumed going out more with Clara. We had discovered clothing stores at SoHo and that made us busy and happy for two whole afternoons. We had also visited Williamsburg looking for a candy store that our teacher had insisted we should visit.

During our conversations, it was inevitable for me to realize how obsessive she was about the idea of forgetting Esteban. She was, indeed, desperately trying to forget him. Maybe that was bothering me so much because I also had someone I wanted to forget. Although I thought I was succeeding in that task, seeing her efforts was making me remind of my own. Everything she had been through so far suddenly made sense to me, from drinking too much, taking drugs, being aggressive towards Mrs. Lupita, and even lacking in concern for her health and her possible state of depression. Our goals were similar, but for me, her actions were being more extreme, and unnecessarily riskier, than mine. We were constantly agreeing and disagreeing, and that was proof that we were acting differently towards our challenges. I was making my own way, and I didn't need to compare it to hers. Without judgment, I started to be less condescending to Clara, always showing my opinions but without arguing. And she finally became less aggressive, and also less bitter. It seemed to me that we had achieved balance in our relationship, and apparently both of us were willing to take advantage of that, in our own way.

Saturday morning, I had coffee with Robert at home. We hadn't shared our day by day in a while, because when I woke up to go to class, he was always still asleep, and when I got up at night he was rarely home. We were used to talk less recently, as we saw each other less.

- Any special plans for tonight? - he asked me, curious.

- I'm meeting some friends to...

- To celebrate your birthday, right? - I found it helpful when he corrected my English, but I didn't like it when he interrupted me.

- Yes, that's right. How do you know? - I asked, aware that I had not mentioned the date to him before.

- I saw it on your profile. - he seemed to enjoy my surprise.

My Profile? What does that mean? Did Robert also access G-Radar? I was momentarily paralyzed, waiting for him to tell me that he was gay and that he had discovered that aspect about me. I didn't want to talk about it with him, as he would certainly make comments full of irony, as usual, and I might not know how to react. Also, I wasn't willing to share more of my life with him, as living under the same roof was already more than enough for me.

- My profile? - I asked, trying to look as little surprised as possible.

- Yes, the one I received from the school, when I found out who was going to rent my room. - he clarified.

- Oh yes. - I couldn't hide the sense of relief. I could see that Robert looked at me differently, as if he had achieved his goal of making me embarrassed.

- So, where is the party?

- We're gonna have dinner at a restaurant on the Upper West Side, Acqua. Do you know it? - I purposefully omitted the rest of the schedule.

- Humm no, I don't. - and fell silent.

- You are invited to go, if you want to! - I felt obliged to invite him, pretending to be excited, but hoping for him to refuse.

- Unfortunately, I can't. But enjoy! And behave yourself! - he said.

- Do you think I haven't been behaving properly? - I replied, curious to hear his answer.

- I'm sure you have. - he replied, smiling and giving me a kiss on the forehead, as was his behavior pattern with me, and then left for his bedroom.

I wondered if I had let him realize the falseness with which I made the invitation. I didn't mean to treat him badly, but I couldn't fit him in my new way of life. He hardly shared his stories with me, wanting to talk exclusively what I had done during the days. Where he was used to spend his days was a mystery to me, and somehow, I didn't feel comfortable asking. I knew that he had traveled a lot during his life, due to the work of his father who had been an airplane pilot, and that whenever he had changed airlines and countries, he had taken his family with him. He also told me that he was often taking small jobs as a freelance lawyer, as well as teaching private English classes to foreign students at a few Manhattan colleges. However, he had not clarified to me which of these jobs were keeping him busy during the days, or why he was constantly out, often entrusting the apartment to me. So, despite the lack of intimacy even though we were living under the same roof, I preferred to continue that way, as I did not like the idea of having another unstable character so close to me. It had already been difficult to strike a balance with Clara. That thought sounded a little bit egoistical in my head but maybe that was what was missing about my new personality, since the old Vicente was used to put everybody's feelings and needs before his.

Saturday night, I arrived at Acqua alone. Outside, the cold was intense, but inside the restaurant the atmosphere was very pleasant. In every way. Clara, Akihiro, and four other colleagues, two from Spain, one from Russia and one from Brazil, were waiting for me to celebrate. Those six people made me laugh for hours, while we tasted typical Italian dishes and appreciated delicious wines. I felt the alcohol rise right after dessert, a chocolate cake that Clara had made to the special occasion, with twenty-seven candles that I blew out. Then, I told my guests we were going to G-Lounge, but besides Clara only the Brazilian boy wanted to follow us. The rest of my colleagues politely declined the invitation.

João was three years younger than me, and he had started at Diplomacy three weeks earlier. Because of the same language, we soon got closer and he became part of some lunches that were previously exclusively mine and Clara's. I felt that she was a little jealous of him, even suggesting that he was interested in me. But I thought that in fact he was interested in her. Very handsome, black curly hair and bright green eyes, he was an attractive guy and had a great conversation, but I never felt for him anything more than friendship. In fact, I wasn't even sure he was gay. I was hoping to find that out that night, after all he must have known that the bar we were going to was a LGBTQ+ place.

We arrived at G-Lounge and the place was crowded. Many beautiful people, even more interesting and charming than Splash's regulars. The decor was predominantly white and silver, giving the impression that we were somewhere in the future. The bar counter was all made of transparent glass, and muscular bartenders dressed in white garments were preparing drinks in bright neon colors. The entire space could easily serve as the scenario for a science fiction movie, set in the year of 2050.

Clara and I approached the bar, while João excused himself to go to the restroom.

- He already realized this place is gay, right? - I asked Clara, who seemed even more cheerful than I was.

- If he didn't notice yet, he will notice in the restroom. - she laughed.

João found us again when we got our drinks. Mine, a very bright blue liquid in a long thin glass, and Clara's, a pink gradient in a modern goblet. We waited for João to order a beer, and then we toasted. For my birthday and for our future.

On the dancefloor, João came closer to me.

- Vicente, I have something to tell you. - he seemed hesitant.

- I knew it. You like boys, right? - I said, sure of my suspicion.

- Yes, I like boys... too. But I thought you've already found that out. - he said, smiling. - It's something else. - he said more seriously.

At that moment, I thought about Clara's jokes and realized that they could be true, he could be attracted to me.

- Ok, what is it? - I asked, already predicting the answer.

- I'm into... Clara.

- What? - I asked, in Portuguese. Until then we had spoken exclusively in English with each other, as we had agreed to train the language. My shock was such that I remembered Portuguese was my native language. - But didn't you just admit you're gay? - I continued, in English.

- I'm bi, Vicente. And I'm very much into Clara. - he clarified.

Clara continued to look at us, believing that her suspicions about his love interest were true, and not suspecting at all that his target was actually her.

- What do you want me to do? Do you want me to tell her? - I offered.

- No, no. I'm shy but I want to do it myself. I just wanted to ask you to leave us alone for a moment, since she doesn't let go of you. - he said, laughing.

- Of course! - I turned to Clara - I'm going to the restroom!

I moved away from them and sat on one of the sofas in the large lounge area, which gave the place its name. I remained there looking at them and hoping for them to kiss. The night was due for enjoyment, and if *I* didn't find someone to have a good time with, those two could do it for me. I liked the idea of João and Clara together. He could be a good company for her. He was nice, responsible, and very handsome. They talked for a while, and the kiss didn't take long to happen, but not before Clara winked at me.

The lounge overlooked a large artificial garden full of colorful and exotic flowers, lit by spotlights enhancing the colors of that lying nature. But being a false nature did not make the beauty of the scenery less extravagant, on the contrary, it had been my only opportunity to contemplate flowers and plants so exuberant in the cold autumn of New York. My blue drink was already over, so I thought about getting up and ordering another one at the bar, when a man dressed all in white crossed my vision. At first, I thought it was someone from the staff of G-Lounge, after all the outfit would make sense like a uniform. But when I saw him sitting next to me, I realized that he was not an employee but a customer, just like me. I sensed a sweet perfume in the air, possibly his. So, I looked to the side to see him better. He was staring at me. The moment our eyes met I felt butterflies in my stomach. *Who was this man?*

- I like your vest. - he said. I was wearing a black vest over a white shirt, black pants and brown boots. I had seen that look in a fashion magazine a few days earlier and decided to reproduce it on my birthday.

- Thanks. - I said to him. - I like your look, too. - I amended. After first mistaken him for a local employee, I realized how beautiful his garments were and how well they were fitting him. Despite a white shirt similar to mine, he wore white pants and a very light blue scarf. He looked almost like an angel.

- I was feeling satisfied about it when I left my house. But now I feel like part of the bar, a continuation of the decor! - he said, laughing. Only then I could realize the perfection of his teeth and the grace of his smile. And also, his muscular figure drawn under the shirt, his strong but well cared hands, and his piercing eyes.

- I think your outfit matches more the theme than mine. I feel like I'm a cowboy out of place. - I tried to be funny, following his cue.

- Well, you missed the hat... - he said, joining the game.

- Yeah! - I laughed more, enjoying the pleasure of that conversation.

- My name is Peter.

- Mine is Vicente, nice to meet you.

- Nice to meet you too. Can I buy you a drink?

- Yes, please. - we got up and went to the bar.

João and Clara weren't where I had left them, I realized at a glance. Peter asked me what I was drinking, and I replied, immediately remembering that I had ordered that blue drink to make fun of Clara. He asked the bartender for my drink and a beer.

- Wow, this is really blue! - He said, handing me the drink.

- It's meant to match your scarf. - I replied. He smiled.

We spent the next two hours talking. I found out, among other things, that he was born in New York, was almost ten years older than me, was the oldest brother of three, was close to his family which he saw regularly despite living in another state, worked in Marketing, had recently moved to a loft in SoHo, preferred dogs to cats, and loved ice cream. He learned, among other things, that I was living temporarily in the city to study English, that I was there with two schoolmates, that I was also close to my family, also preferred dogs to cats, and also loved ice cream.

- Many things in common. - he observed.

- Yes. - I agreed, unable to rip the smile off my face.

- And what brought you and your colleagues to this bar today?

- My birthday.

- Wow, happy birthday! If I knew I would've bought you something... - he was being funny.

- You can give me a gift later. - I was being myself, funny as was I used to be.

- I sure will. - another charming smile.

- In the meantime, shall we dance a little?

- Of course! - he grabbed my hands and guided me to the dance-floor.

We danced to songs that seemed made for that moment. Each one of them fit perfectly, for the lyrics that spoke of joy, passion and party, or for the melody that allowed us to dance separately or together, perfect nesting our bodies. I started to believe that he was indeed an angel because I was feeling like I was in heaven.

- Vicente, unfortunately I need to go now. I have to work tomorrow. - he said, after we left the dancefloor and went back to the lounge to sit down.

I thought about what to say for a moment, torn between *No, stay!* and *Ok, no problem.* I didn't want to look needy, like Raul, but I also didn't want to look careless, like Pierre. I decided to stay in the middle.

- Wow, I shouldn't have held you that long, then. - I regretted it the instant I said it. It looked tacky. But he didn't seem to care.

- No problem, actually I thank you for holding me. Every minute was worth it. Will you accompany me to the door?

We went down the stairs that led us to the exit, and before reaching the door, he gave me a hug and a long kiss, making me shiver. A good shiver.

- I want to see you again. - he said.

- Of course. - I agreed, feeling happy.

We exchanged our phone numbers, and then he was gone. I went upstairs again, planning to find João and Clara. When I got up there, my cell beeped. A message.

I had an idea for your gift. Tell me if Tuesday is a good day for you. XXX, Peter - the one in white :)

I smiled at the phone screen. Then I felt a nudge in the back, so turned and saw Clara with a curious look.

- What is it?

- You won't believe it! - I said.

- Oh yeah? So, tell me!

- I will! But first, where is João?

- At the bar, waiting for another beer.

- You didn't suspect anything about him? - I asked.

- I don't know. Sometimes I thought he was throwing his charm at me, but as I was also suspicious that he was gay I thought the charm was actually for you! I never imagined he was bi.

- Me neither! So...what happened?

- Well...there was this fantastic chemistry! We kissed and it seemed that everything made sense! - she smiled.

- I'm so happy for you. For you two! - I said.

- Yeah, let's take it easy, right... you know how difficult I am. - she grinned.

- Yes, I know! I'll let him know, ok? - we laughed.

- Ok, but today is your day! Come on, tell me where have you been all this time?

Still waiting for João to arrive, I told Clara everything quickly but in details. I thought that I wouldn't feel comfortable talking about Peter to João. Also, with Clara I wouldn't have to explain certain things for the story to make sense, because of our intimacy. I managed to finish the story before he approached us.

- So, you look like you enjoyed your time alone, huh? - said João.

- Let's say I did! - I replied, slightly embarrassed, but very satisfied.

- Dude, this club is awesome! Shall we dance more?

- Yeah, let's do it. - I agreed. And the three of us went back to the dancefloor.

The night was long, and every moment felt magical. Maybe because it was my birthday, maybe because I met Peter, or even because I had the feeling that Clara was once again my good old friend. Regardless of all, one thing I knew for sure, on that day a new chapter had started.

CHAPTER VIII

- What took you so long to have a birthday, huh, Vicente? - asked Clara, during our brunch at Pax. My favorite time to visit Times Square used to be on Sunday mornings, as there were fewer people and the sunlight seemed brighter even with the billboards on. However, that day there were more tourists than usual, after all the Thanksgiving holiday was approaching, and it would be followed by Christmas and other New Year's celebrations, occasions that traditionally bring more visitors to Manhattan.

- Well, I can't choose the day of my birthday! Besides, everything has its time, Clara. - I replied.

- Yeah, it's true. Just like my story with João.

- Oh yeah? Your story with João? What story? - I laughed, making fun of her.

- Are you jealous?

- Of course not, I'm happy for you two. And I'm about to get one story for myself too. - I joked, thinking unpretentiously about Peter.

We both laughed. That was our best date in weeks, and we both realized that our friendship was finally back to normal. There was no need to say anything, neither apologize nor demand explanations.

Peace was reigning over us. After the brunch we went for a walk in Central Park.

The park was beautifully showing its almost leafless trees, suggesting the famous landscape of photos and films of a Central Park with a winter face. We walked down a stone path to a bridge and stopped to admire the view of some tall buildings appearing more clearly through the twisted branches of the trees.

- Vicente, there are still some tourist spots for us to visit. - said Clara, referring to our deal.

- We can go somewhere this week, before the city receives more visitors. What do you think?

- Good idea!... - she replied in a tone suggesting there was something more she would like to say.

- What is it? - I asked.

- Nothing...it's just... - she hesitated.

- You can tell me, Clara.

- Well, when we made our deal, we agreed to be just you and me, right?

- Yes, and?

- And I was wondering if João could join us. - she said, looking embarrassed. Then continued, almost stumbling over her words - I know that both you and I had our love problems before coming here, and that we have been trying to overcome this, and putting other guys into our deal might not be a good idea, and...

- Listen, Clara. - I interrupted her. - You told me you were trying to find someone who could make you forget Esteban. Whether João is that person or not, only time will tell. But if you wanna try, I am extremely happy to help. And I don't bother including him in our activities! He is a nice guy and I like his company.

- Thank you, Vicente! - she said, hugging me.

- And let me tell you, I'm glad you considered my opinion, because, let's face it, lately you've been different, and I was afraid that our friendship was at risk - I came clear with her.

- Vicente, I don't know what was happening to me. I felt vulnerable, really lost. And talking about it bothered me, even if it were with you. So, I apologize for that. And I mean it.

- Wow, João really did you good, huh? - I joked, happy with the apology.

- Yeah, he did. But it wasn't just him. I've had a bad time in these past few weeks. I met people who seemed cool to me and who turned out to be real idiots. I made bad choices, but I am aware of that. And I want to start again. João can help me, but I feel it inside me, regardless of him.

- That's great. And I'm sorry if I ever judged you or tried to make you follow my rules. I also felt vulnerable, but I think it was part of our growth, right? - I hugged her again. I was feeling strangely fulfilled, after all I was hoping we could have that conversation for weeks.

On the subway, coming home that night, I thought about what we had talked about, and it still made me happy, hours later. Looking at the horizontal signage of stations above one of the subway doors, I realized that the light that indicated the 168th Street station, which had been broken and off for weeks, had been replaced and was shining bright again. Clara's path, like that station, had become clearer. When my cell beeped and a message from Peter appeared, I opened it to read.

How is the hottest Brazilian I had ever met? Can we meet Tuesday at 5:30 pm in my apartment? I'll send the address later! X, Peter.

I smiled involuntarily, mainly because of the compliment in the message. It was inevitable to relate that good feeling to what Clara was having with João. We had both met someone who had touched us in a different, special way. And that night Clara realized how much she could gain from that relationship, even though she claimed that an internal change had also happened. Would it be okay for me to bond with Peter? Could that take me away from my goals? Or help me achieve them?

- Are you close? - asked Peter over the phone.

- Yes, crossing the street. - I replied.

- Okay, ring the bell. Apartment 404.

- Right! - I hung up the call.

It was Tuesday, and at 5:30 pm sharp I was arriving at Peter's, as agreed. I was curious about meeting him again to see if what I remembered about him was real or result of my expectations, based on the few hours we spent together at the club days ago.

- I'm glad you're here. - he said smiling, as he opened the door. It was the loft of my dreams. A large space probably used by a factory in the past, with apparent plumbing, walls with bricks and rustic paint, varnished cement floor, and minimalist, although cozy, decor. Only the bedroom and bathroom were separated by walls and doors. And the view was impressive. From the two wide windows in the living room it was possible to see part of SoHo, and from the kitchen window, the south of the island with its silhouette of large and imposing buildings. Peter received me with a hug, a long kiss, and we went to the kitchen, where he was preparing us a homemade pasta with organic tomato sauce.

- If I could, I would only eat natural food, like this one. - I said.

- What prevents you from doing it? - asked me.

- Mc Donald's, Burger King, Pizza Hut... - I said, laughing.

- I understand you. I also let myself be carried away from time to time by junk food, it's easier, right? But I don't give up. Whenever I can, I prepare my meals.

- I admire that. - I said, really enjoying Peter's philosophy of life, as well as his gorgeous kitchen, his company, and the soft music that came from his iPhone coupled to a state-of-the-art dock in the living room.

While we waited for the sauce to reduce over low heat, we sat in the living room and Peter poured me a glass of wine. He told me that he had bought the apartment at a price below the market because the owner was in a hurry to sell it, since he was moving to California. It would be the first Christmas Peter would spend there, and for that reason he had invited some long-time friends who lived far from him to celebrate the occasion together. As he told his stories, I realized how much he had achieved in his professional life without his personal life being left aside, and how important his values were to him. I began to nurture an admiration for who Peter was as a person, in addition to his very handsome and well-groomed figure, and also for the ability to put me at ease in the face of that kind of situation, of being for the first time at someone's home.

Dish ready, we sat at the table to eat. The meal was delicious, as was the continuation of our getting-to-know-each-other chat. I told him about my situation with Clara and how things were back to normal. I also talked about my work as a photographer and he asked me to see some of it. I took out my phone and showed him photos of the last two exhibitions I had held in Brazil.

- Vicente, your point of view is impeccable. - he said. - And you have a latent sensitivity.

- Thanks. - I was glad to have won that compliment.

- I would like to have a piece by you here in my apartment. One of your photographs in one of my walls.

- Gosh, it would be an honor. - I got more flattered.

Whether the food and the compliments had been a ploy to win me over or just Peter being himself I didn't know, but I felt totally involved. After another glass of wine, listening to a jazz CD that he had placed to show me one of his favorite singers, we went to the bedroom. No movement during the night seemed forced, on the contrary, seemed to be part of the script for a perfect date. The touch of his hands on my body made me shiver, just like during our first kiss. His scent anesthetized me and transported me to a state of relaxation in which I had not been in a long time. Our bodies found perfect fit and the pleasure I felt by being there extended beyond orgasm. When I regained my full consciousness, we were still lying naked in his bed.

- So, was that my gift? - I asked, still excited.

- Part of it. - he replied. - On Saturday we will have dinner and I will give you the other part. What do you say?

- Humm... - I pretended to think, to make fun. - OK, deal. - I replied, smiling.

I spent that night in Peter's loft. We slept with our arms around each other.

During the following days, I had the first tests at level 7, the highest of Diplomacy. With the focus being conversation and vocabulary, the exams included essays on controversial topics such as abortion and pedophilia, and matters that seemed ironically convenient for me, such as homosexuality, prejudice and the future of human relationships. The school's goal was to get students to practice the use of unusual words, and to be able to develop convincing and well-structured dissertations on subjects that are difficult to comprehensively discuss using a new language. I was tested not only for English proficiency, but also for my ability to elaborate an opinion on these issues, especially the last two. I had the feeling that I had left more questions than answers on the test sheets, and when I got them back with the assessment, I realized I was right. I needed to continue my search for explanations, but I still had time to do it. Specially out of school.

On Saturday I went to dinner with Peter in Little Italy, in a restaurant that reminded me of old Italian movies. I had never been to Italy, but I felt like I was in Rome. Another delicious meal, and we went to the front of the restaurant.

- I don't wanna look anxious, but you promised me the second part of my gift. - I said to Peter, smiling and playing with my hand on his.

- Fair enough! Shall we? - he asked, hailing a taxi.

A few minutes later, we were in front of a Broadway theater. Chicago was on show, and a line was taking shape at the entrance.

- We're going to see a musical? - I asked, excited.

- Yes! You said you like musicals, right?

- I love them! Thank you, Peter. - I kissed him.

- Calm down, thank me later. - he said, with the look of someone who is up to something.

I had already seen two shows since my arrival in New York, so going to a Broadway theater was not news for me. But there were two important differences. One of them was that I wasn't alone, like the other times. And the other one, I realized immediately when we got out of the car. We didn't stop at the box office entrance, so I thought Peter had already arranged the tickets. Instead, we entered through a side door guarded by a security. The moment the guard closed the door behind us, I understood that we were behind the scenes.

- Peter, are we...

- Backstage? Yes. - he completed my question and answered it.

- But how...? - I tried to ask, surprised.

- You'll understand.

We walked down a dimly lit corridor, with walls full of posters of past shows, and a strong scent of perfume, until we reached a wooden door with a sign. A male name and a star glued to the bottom indicated that that was a dressing room, from one of the stars of that Chicago montage.

- Great Peter! - exclaimed Ben, as soon as we entered.

- How are you, my friend? This is Vicente. - he said, hugging me closely.

- Nice to meet you. - I said, still startled.

Peter and Ben had studied together in high school and had never distanced themselves. Great friends, Ben always booked a session of his shows for Peter to watch him. That day, I would join Peter in the front row.

I was able to see the preparation of the actors before going on stage, the applying of the strong makeup, the vocal warm-up, the stretching for the dance. It was like being part of the show.

I had seen the movie Chicago, so I already knew most of the songs. But seeing the musical live from a short distance, close to the orchestra and the actors, allowed the beats of the songs to have another meaning for me. The story of the musical was not at all similar to mine, but I was able to identify myself with several aspects of the montage. The scenery was composed only by the musicians and a dark background. Each song was packed with firm numbers of tap dancing, high-pitched voices and sensual dances that took over and decorated the stage, taking the place of great structures seen in other musicals. Despite the comedy present in almost the entire duration of the show, which was usually the great catch for the viewer's attention, it was the tension that caught my attention. The world depicted on-stage was a clear game of lies, in black and white. Real life used to have more nuances, more duality and less contrast. It was easy to see how art imitates life, but it gives it a sense of its own, a more resolved one. I wasn't actually part of the show, I was there offstage, and sud-denly I found myself wanting to give my life a sense of its own too. For a moment, a film crossed my mind, with events from the past and things I had experienced in the previous two months. Being away from everything and everyone I had contact with in my life was re-vealing, because some aspects prior to the trip did not make sense to me, even before and much less at that moment. I felt that in New York I was genuinely achieving things for the first time in my life. I felt powerful, just like the dancers who stamped their feet on the floor and followed the noise with their palms. I felt that my emotions were more on the edge, like a cello string that cried when played by the bow during a sad song. And I realized how fearless I could be about life, in the same way that actors moved from shadow to light, courageously, during a dance.

I came back to reality with the public's ovation at the end of the show.

- You can thank me now. - said Peter, with a big smile on his lips.

- Thank you *very* much. - I said, hugging him and wanting to cry. He probably didn't understand why I was so emotional at that mo-ment, but it didn't matter, I knew why.

Thanksgiving Day had arrived, and we would meet at João's apartment to celebrate. Clara and I spent the morning on one of the corners of Seventh Avenue, watching Macy's parade, marveling at each big inflatable balloon that appeared up in the sky, between the buildings. Clara looked like a child, excited about children's characters, especially her favorite, Hello Kitty. After the parade, we went skating in Central Park. I had never skated on ice, which proved to be a difficulty due to my lack of balance and the cold of that afternoon. The temperature was getting lower each day and staying outdoors for a long time was becoming uncomfortable.

In the middle of the afternoon I took the subway to Washington Heights to take a shower, change clothes and go to meet João, Clara and some other colleagues for our supper. Arriving home, I realized that Robert was not there, but had left a note on my bed.

Do you still live with me? :) Tomorrow night, I will decorate the Christmas tree and would like your company. Tell me if you can, okay? R.

After the previous night, and the bold energy that the musical had brought me, I had decided not to avoid Robert anymore, after all it was getting harder to find him at home anyway. The invitation seemed interesting and we had spent no time together for a while, so I decided to accept it. I wrote *Ok, of course, count on me! V* on the same note, under his signature, and went to get myself ready to go out.

At 8:30 pm I arrived at João's apartment. Everyone was already there, some of them playing Twister. I joined Clara and João, who were in the kitchen preparing Brussels sprouts, mashed potatoes, cranberry sauce and a big turkey.

- We'll have a traditional supper, Vicente! - said João excitedly.

- I see! Do you need help?

- No, thanks! Help yourself a glass of wine and go play with the others. - said Clara.

I went on into the living room and joined Twister with three other colleagues. At certain times, I looked into the kitchen and saw the two interacting like a real couple, happy to prepare a meal together. That made me overjoyed. Later, we met at the table to eat. Everyone gave thanks for some aspect of life, according to the tradition we had learned at school. In general, everyone talked about the experience in living in the city. I could see that I was not the only one in New York looking for answers and a new attitude towards life. When it was Clara's turn, I was curious to see what she was going to say.

- I give thanks to New York for making me repeat some mistakes of the past, and for giving me the opportunity to do it right from now on. - she started, emotional. - And I thank João for being one of the best gifts I received this year. Besides Vicente. - and looked at me with affection.

Everyone applauded, and they kissed. It was good to see that Clara was really well. After supper, she pulled me aside.

- Vicente, I have something new to tell you.

- Are you and João getting married? - I asked, jokingly.

- No! - she laughed. - But we're moving in together.

- Wow, that's great news, Clara! - I said excitedly. - But João already has a roommate, and you live with Mrs. Lupita, how are you going to do it?

- Well... - she began, and I realized that there was more news to come. - We're moving to San Francisco.

- What? - I asked, as if I hadn't understood what she had just said to me. I couldn't control my astonishment.

- Yep, we will transfer our classes to the campus there. - she explained.

- But have you seen if this is possible? Have you already searched for apartments? - I asked, involuntarily, trying to understand all the details.

- Yes, Vicente. And don't act like you're my dad, ok? We're both almost the same age! - she said, laughing.

She knew me. She knew I was trying to make her sure of that decision, so as not to take a hurried move. I had done this several times during the past two months, even when we were experiencing our difficulties. But at that moment I felt the decision made sense to her, and that I didn't have to worry.

- You know, Clara, these last few days I have been thinking a lot about our lives here.

- Oh, really? - she made fun of me. - And?

- And I realized, maybe late but not too late, that here we can indeed be whatever we want, whoever we want, as you said on our first date. The secret is just to know that each choice has its consequences and its renunciations. Knowing this, we just have to be brave and go ahead. - I said, living up to the courage I felt.

- So, I was right, huh? - she laughed. - But jokes aside, Vicente, moving in with João seems like the right thing to do, you know?

- Yes, I understand you. And I tell you, if it makes sense, go ahead.

We hugged and Clara cried. I couldn't stop thinking that with her moving, I would have even more free time to decide what to do with the next month that I still had in the city. Would that be good or bad, only time would tell.

CHAPTER IX

Diplomacy was in recess for the Thanksgiving, so I had Friday off. I took the opportunity to walk down Tenth Avenue and reach the Highline Park, to admire the Hudson River. Breathing that humid air reminded me of weekends at the beach, a common hobby for me in Brazil. Whether with my family or friends, whenever I could I went down to the coast to spend a few days. Even though it was chilly that morning, and I didn't even touch the water, being there made me feel refreshed.

After spending some time feeling that breeze, I headed east and stopped in Times Square. I realized that it was the first Friday morning that I visited that area, because on all the others since I arrived in the city, I had had classes. The famous red staircase was not as empty as it was on Sunday mornings, when I liked to sit there and enjoy that place that never stopped. It was an ordinary day, and the place was behaving that way, but with more visitors. I sat on a bench, next to a lady in a big green fake-fur coat. Green was my favorite color.

- Aren't you cold, mister? - she started a conversation, in a gentle and sweet voice.

- Yes, I am. But not as much as you, I suppose. - I replied, smiling. She smiled back. Although the temperature was around five degrees Celsius, I was comfortable with a long-sleeved T-shirt, an overcoat I had bought at a Century 21 sale and a scarf I had won from a great friend prior to the trip. On lesser cold days, I had wrapped up more to get out of the apartment.

- You know, I live here for forty years, and I still haven't gotten used to these low temperatures. - she continued. - My husband's dream was always for us to move to Florida, because of the pleasant weather. - she said, showing sadness in her voice.

- I like warm weather too, but I don't mind this cold. - I said to her.

She remained there, looking up, as if remembering her husband. I didn't want to disturb her, so I went back to enjoy the view, following the hasty passersby crossing the streets, the lively falafel salesmen serving their clients, the many tourists taking lots of pictures with the famous billboards in the background.

- Well, I have to go. - she turned to me again. - Must prepare my lunch. I like to have lunch early, it's good for health. - she said, getting up.

- Ok, have a nice day! - I wished her. She thanked me and disappeared among a group of people who took advantage of the closed signal to cross one of the streets.

The cold was indeed intense, but I really didn't mind it anymore. *I wouldn't trade New York for Florida,* I thought.

After having lunch by myself and spending the afternoon visiting gift shops, I returned home. On the subway, I overheard two gentlemen commenting on the news about a snow forecast for the following weeks. That cheered me up, I could finally see snow up close.

I opened the door and Robert was sitting in the kitchen. I approached him and saw that there were three packages on the table.

- I'm glad you accepted my invitation. - said Robert, with a broad smile. I was touched by his excitement, and I knew that I had done the right thing by deciding to decorate the Christmas tree with him.

- So, let's do it? - I asked, also smiling.

- You can take a shower first, to relax. - he answered. - In the meantime, I'll put these pies in the oven, so we can eat them while we do it. - he said, unwrapping one of the packages and revealing its content, a pumpkin pie. The other two were made of chocolate and almonds, I found out later.

- Good idea. - I said and went to the bathroom.

I showed up at the kitchen ten minutes later, and in addition to the pies and a mug of hot chocolate on the table, I realized that Robert had put a vinyl record with Christmas carols as a soundtrack for our moment. He was in the living room, on a stool, reaching for boxes that were on the top of the wooden shelves.

- Can you help me here, Vicente? - he shouted.

- Sure! - I replied, finishing a sip of hot chocolate.

I helped him down four small and light boxes and a very large and heavy box off the shelf. In the big box was an artificial green pine tree.

- I know that traditionally we have to buy a natural tree, but this pine tree belonged to my grandmother and since she gave it to me just before she died, I use it every Christmas in honor of her. - Robert explained, even though I didn't ask anything.

- And in the smaller boxes you have the ornaments? - I asked.

- Yes. Take the yellow one, the ones in it are the oldest.

I opened the yellow box and found very delicate Christmas balls, made of glass, and appearing to be older than me. One more detailed than the other.

- They are stunning, Robert. - I said. - Aren't you afraid to use and break them? - I remembered when I was a child, and my brothers and me had broken several times the glass balls my mother used to decorate our Christmas tree, because we didn't know how to handle them properly.

- They exist to be used, Vicente. That is the tradition. - he answered.

While Robert was assembling the branches of the artificial pine, I continued to open the small boxes to find more beautiful ornaments. In addition to the colored glass balls, there were golden bells, silver angels, and plastic musical notes decorated with glitter. When I opened the last box, a black one, I noticed that there weren't just Christmas ornaments in it. On top of a golden garland, there was a photo. In it, a younger Robert and a man by his side. The two were embraced, with their heads touching each other, and big smiles on their lips.

- Is this photo also an ornament? - I asked, curious to know its story. That was a great indication that my suspicion about Robert's sexuality was correct. He turned to me, looked at the box, saw the photograph, and looked at me again.

- You got me. - he said, with an embarrassed look.

- How so? - I couldn't resist appearing naïve, like the first time he wanted to bring up the subject. It was stronger than me, and like the other time, as soon as I spoke, I regretted not being more incisive or mature about the situation.

- Well, Vicente, there's something I've been trying to tell you, and I think it's time. - Robert began. - Do you remember the day you got here, and we met two men at the entrance to Fort Tryon?

- Yes. - I replied, sure of what he was getting at.

- You realized that they were not just two friends, right? - he asked me.

- Yes, they were boyfriends. - I said, in an impulse to help him get to the main part of his speech, and in an attempt to stop appearing naïve and alienated about it.

- Exactly. In this picture you can also see boyfriends. - he said, expecting a reaction from me. I looked at the picture again and noticed that Robert was at least ten years younger. I thought about what to say to him.

- Well, boyfriends or ex-boyfriends? - I tried to make fun, to break the tension that was beginning to grow.

- Ex-boyfriends. - replied Robert, starting to laugh softly. - Did you ever imagine that I... you know?

- Yes, and I am too. - I said, and I was surprised by the ease I was feeling in opening up to him. It had been even easier than it was with

Clara. But I suspected that I had done it to look even less naïve and more confident, prouder of my condition.

- I thought so. - he said. - Well, we have one more topic to discuss, then, right?

Revealing to each other that we were both gay was enough for me, I didn't want to make this similarity a reason for us to be more intimate. But it didn't take long for him to start talking about how he had discovered himself in childhood, and how difficult it had been to live with that condition in a traditional family like his. Until that moment no family member had known about this aspect about him, and he had only managed to lead a *normal* life in that regard after moving to New York and meeting Ted, the guy in the picture, fifteen years earlier. They had lived together in that apartment for six years, until Robert discovered he was being cheated. Despite forgiving the betrayal, Ted had chosen to end the relationship and move out. While Robert was telling me each part of it, I noticed, in his speech, a grudge that was still present and also a great disappointment about love. I asked him if he had suffered after Ted's departure, and he said that he did, but that then he had started attending the church he had taken me to, and that that had made his heart filled again. It was evident that he had relied in part of his faith to cure a disappointment, but it was also clear that he was very frustrated by the city, the scenario of his broken-hearted story. I remembered his speech at the restaurant, at our first meal together, when he said that the city was full of promises that could not be kept. *Did Robert go to New York hoping to find great love, as many other people do?*

- Have you been in a relationship, Vicente? - he asked me, after finishing his story.

- Yes. - I replied. - I was kind of dating a guy before coming here.

- Well, I could tell. - he said. - When you told me you came here with goals, but did not specify them, I sensed that you had an unfinished love story.

- I wouldn't say that forgetting my ex-boyfriend was the main reason for me to take this trip. - I said, reluctant to agree with him, although knowing inside that that was true.

- Vicente, let's face it. You all come here for the same reason. I came too. But it is not true, the city does not keep its promises. - he began to badmouth Manhattan again. I avoided interrupting him. He continued. - What really works is believing in something bigger, in something real, as our church preaches. And then you start to give less importance to relationships. You saw that day yourself, and you liked it. I think you should attend our meetings more, it will help you.

I suddenly found myself facing a person who was telling me that I needed help, that I had problems, and that he magically had the solutions. I agreed that love was complicated and that in life it was useful to believe in something greater, but one thing did not necessarily have to do with the other. Besides, who was he to judge me or tell me what was right or wrong? He was not an example for me, and after that, he hardly would be. I considered telling him that the solution he had found had worked for him, but that it was not mandatorily the rule. But I thought it best not to contradict him. I did have an unresolved story with someone in my past, but I was not hopeless about finding someone better in my future. In fact, in my present there was already someone very nice. However, I didn't want to share that with Robert.

I changed the subject and we finished decorating the tree.

Lying on my inflatable bed at night, I thought again about everything Robert had told me. I understood his life story, shaped by prejudice and difficulty of acceptance, but denial was not a path in which I allowed myself to walk through, and for me, that was what he was doing. All the bitterness of his broken heart had been masked by new beliefs about life, supported by a version of his faith that canceled out one of the most important points of his own religion: love.

CHAPTER X

Back in class, I met with Clara at Diplomacy while choosing a cereal bar at one of the school's vending machines. To my surprise she had taken the exam to level up and got a spot in my class. We were classmates again, at least for another fifteen days, before she left for Florida.

- Vicente, before moving I want to visit one last tourist attraction with you. - she said.

- Yep, of course. - I agreed. - What do you think about The Top Of The Rock? - I suggested.

- Great! We should go at night, since we went to The Empire State during the day.

- Great idea. Let's just hope we don't get a long line. - I said.

And we took the longest line of all our visits, the following night. João was unable to accompany us, so we considered that activity to be the last officially together, just the two of us, Vicente and Clara.

From above, the city seemed to be lit up by huge spotlights from the sky. It was as if the clouds hid the source of the spots, even though they were there, all facing the city. Getting close to the glass parapet on the second floor of the observatory was not an easy task given the number of visitors, but once leaning against the edge of the building we stood there for a while, talking to each other. Regardless of the subjects, the atmosphere of the conversation was of farewell. The city's famous bright lights were witnesses of that moment. Our friendship had been born, had grown up, had had its conflicts, had grown stronger and was now reaching a place still unknown, but very gratifying.

- We won't stop talking after I leave, right? - questioned Clara.

- Of course not! - I confirmed, although not sure. I didn't know if our friendship would overcome the distance, but I was happy for what we had already lived, and I didn't want to spoil that moment by being pessimistic.

We took a selfie together, with New York beautifully lit in the background, to keep that moment registered not only in our memories but in a photograph.

After descending the tower, already on one of the benches next to The Rockefeller Center skating rink, we said goodbye. Clara left for João's apartment, and I left for Peter's apartment.

Entering the loft, I noticed a different lighting. Candles everywhere. Peter was waiting for me holding two glasses of wine in his hands. He had again cooked a delicious dinner for us, and had made his home the most romantic setting I had ever been in. It was not difficult to get carried away by the atmosphere and spend all night having sex.

The following Tuesday, I joined Clara on her last visit to a souvenir shop to buy gifts for some of her family members. She would stay in Florida for three months and had at that moment more memorabilia from the United States than me, who was about to leave for Brazil. Looking at some key chains in the shape of traditional yellow cabs, a postcard beside them caught my attention. Made of a kind of holographic material, depending on the angle it was held, it was possible to read *I Love New York* and *New York Loves Me*. That image awoke something in me.

On my arrival, full of expectations about the city, all built on cinematographic references, I had been greatly influenced by the warning Robert had given me regarding the promises of the city. Since then I had been trying to identify the real image of the city, what it really represented for me. Without realizing, I had been holding myself from loving the city. And probably because of Robert's opinion about it. I had recently understood that his frustration had a reason, and that it was coming from a place similar to mine. But I refused using the same approach as him. I had my own religion, I believed in something bigger, but I especially believed in love.

In that moment, I decided that I was prepared to love New York - as the t-shirts from that souvenir store were suggesting.

- Clara, do you remember when you asked me why I've chosen New York?

- Yes, of course. Do you have an answer now?

- I don't think I've chosen it. I think I was chosen.

Clara nodded, and smiled at me.

After more than eighty days in the city, I bought my first t-shirt proclaiming to the world my love. And I hoped that the city would love me too, as the postcard suggested.

I arrived for Clara's farewell at Five Guys on 55th Street the following night, by myself. That's how I've been walking lately, and it didn't bother me at all. She had chosen to eat hamburger and fries on her last night, as a tribute to the American cuisine. For her, in Florida the style would be different, healthier. Besides Clara and João there were some other colleagues from Diplomacy, including Akihiro. After everyone ordered their snacks and sat down, Clara and I were still waiting at the counter.

- I'll never forget our love affair, Vicente! - she said, smiling but with tears in her eyes. - New York wouldn't be the same without you. I love you, my friend!

- I love you too, *loca!* - I dared to speak a little bit of Spanish. We hugged.

The night ended with a lot of laughter, and I thought it was good that I could remember her that way. Clara had achieved her goal. She had managed to forget her old boyfriend and now she could move on to a new phase of discovery. She had been important to my story in that place, just as Robert had been, and Peter was being. However, the reason for my trip was not restricted to working on the disappointment of an unresolved love affair. That was only part of it, and now I could take it on without fear. There was still the goal of knowing how to live alone, which I felt I was reaching day by day, and the discovery of who was the real Vicente. That last one would be my next mission. And conquering it was entirely up to me.

Peter was going to travel on business for a few days, which would leave me with no reason not to sleep at home. The few times that Robert and I met after the day of setting up the Christmas tree were quick, and it was clear that he was trying to talk more about matters other than school, especially his new favorite: his homosexuality. Just like the night he told me his life story, whenever we saw each other, even for a few minutes, he loved to comment on this topic, almost always sarcastically as if trying to get a laugh from me. But regardless of the situation, I no longer found the urge to discuss this subject with him, since I didn't want to go into details about me and Peter. I was not sure why I was feeling this reservation towards Robert, but maybe it was due to the excess of irony in his speech. So, I chose to keep my intimacy confined to me and omit certain passages when he questioned me about my days.

That was the first night I went back to sleep at home, after days away. Despite knowing that I would have Robert's company, I was excited to spend a few nights back at my old home, and to be able to analyze the whole situation around what I was living with Peter. I wanted to make sure that the excitement I felt when we first met still prevailed over the convenience of having a place outside Robert's apartment where I could spend my nights. After arriving, taking a shower and shutting myself in my room, I started to think about the latest events. Yes, I was enjoying Peter's company far beyond convenience. Yes, I would miss Clara, but I was able to survive the city and my new lifestyle alone. And no, I wouldn't let the discomfort with Robert ruin the cozy feeling I had about that apartment, which had become my home almost three months ago. In the midst of these ramblings, Robert knocked on the door. I opened it, he came in and we sat on one of the sofas.

- Christmas is coming. - he said.

- Yes, time went by so fast... - I said.

- And what are your plans for Christmas Eve? - he asked.

I had thought days ago that he could ask me that question, and I was trying to come up with my own plans so that there was no possibility for him to invite me to his, whatever it would be. But I couldn't think of anything.

- Nothing yet. - I was forced to admit. Some Diplomacy colleagues were talking about having dinner at a restaurant, but I wasn't excited to join them.

- Well, I have an invitation for you.

Another invitation? I thought, a little bit tense but curious.

- An invitation for...?

- There will be a party Midtown at the apartment of two friends of mine and I would like you to go with me. It's a traditional party, they do it every year and invite very interesting people. What do you think?

- Actually, a group of school colleagues is organizing a dinner... - I started, thinking about refusing his invitation at the end of my sentence. *A party of two of his friends?* Robert hadn't introduced me to a single friend, not even talked about one. *What if that event was boring?* He interrupted me.

- I guarantee you will not regret it if you go. - he said, taking one of my hands. - They always set up a big tree in the middle of the room, and everyone bring ornaments to decorate it, it is very beautiful. And one of them is a chef, so the food is always wonderful. Come on, Vicente? - he asked me.

- I would have to talk to my colleagues... - I lied.

- Please, come with me. At least this last time, before you leave back home.

I couldn't refuse. He had a point, soon I would be leaving and maybe that was a good way to say goodbye to our activities together. Also, the way he was looking at me seemed as inviting as the first time we met, with his very blue eyes. I remembered that nice and promising Robert, although this time he seemed more needy and less caring.

- Okay, I'll go with you. From what you say, it'll be quite a party. - I pretended excitement. *Maybe the party wouldn't be boring.* And maybe it would be good to do something different than spend more time with my colleagues. After all, Christmas had always been a rather sad date for me, for no special reason. I would rather do a new activity than try to reproduce the family dinner as I had been doing all the past years, because then it would be sad.

The days until Christmas Eve passed slowly. Although I was enjoying doing activities on my own, I had fewer appointments at school or with Peter. Clara was gone, and I didn't feel totally connected to the new colleagues at Diplomacy, so the time seemed to go by much more dragged. I visited the MoMA for inspiration on future photographic work. I discovered a Japanese clothing store with very interesting items. I walked around several *Walgreens* looking for cosmetic products that would solve the problem of dry mouth caused by the cold. I watched movies that premiered in the major theaters such as Regal and AMC. I was loving the city and was giving it the opportunity to love me back, for what I was.

So, it was the twenty-fourth of December. I woke up late taking advantage of the fact that the school was in recess due to the holiday. Robert stayed out all morning and I took the opportunity to prepare something to eat, take a shower and go for a walk around the neighborhood. It had been a long time since I had enjoyed the vicinity.

The weather seemed colder than ever, and I had to go out with a scarf and a wool hat. Fort Tryon Park was even prettier with its trails covered with dry brown leaves, and the view of the Hudson River was particularly pleasant. The blue tones of the water allowed me to take very good photos, and I thought that scenery would give me a great exhibit material. I returned home late in the afternoon, close to the time I had agreed to meet with Robert at the apartment, to get ready and go to the party.

- The forecast is for snow tonight! - Robert shouted as soon as I walked in the door.

- Oh really? - I said, really excited.

- Yes! Wouldn't that be romantic? - he said, laughing.

- The perfect setting for a Christmas movie. - I imagined out loud.

- Well, I'm going to take a shower and then you can go, okay? - he said.

- Okay. - I agreed.

While he used the bathroom, I called my parents and wished them a Merry Christmas. It was already night in Brazil, and they were meeting with many of my family members, as usual. A part of me wished to be with them at that moment, but I held that feeling and hung up the phone before I started to cry.

Robert came out of the bathroom groomed in a way that I had never seen him. He usually wore baggy pants, loose t-shirts and threw a dull brown coat on top of everything when he went out into the street. For that occasion, he had chosen formal trousers, a distinctive white shirt, a vest, a bow tie and a beret. I couldn't help smiling when I saw him. He was very nice and graceful in that look.

- You're committed to the look, huh? - I teased.

- Yes, tonight will be an unforgettable evening. - he said.

Obviously less engaged than him, I expected it to be at least nice.

We arrived at the apartment of Robert's friends. He hadn't told me before, but the couple was quite wealthy, and the place was huge. Many guests were standing in the main room and some inside the kitchen area and other surroundings. As I was told, there was a big tree in the middle of the room. It was the largest Christmas tree I had ever seen. Green, natural and with many ornaments of all sizes and styles, without compromising its good look. I walked over and hung a red-and-white striped candy cane that I had bought earlier at a Fort Tryon Park store. Robert's friends came to greet us. A gay couple. Ross and Kyle had met Robert on a trip to Morocco and had traveled together every year since then. Very friendly, but visibly busy with the party tasks, they showed us where the buffet was and went to greet new guests who were arriving.

Robert and I walked through the rooms of the dazzling apartment, helped ourselves to a glass of punch, and went to a closed balcony, from where it was possible to see much of the north of the island, after all we were on the twenty-second floor. There, Robert met another friend and the two of them started a lively conversation. I took the opportunity to mingle throughout the other guests.

The party's audience was mainly formed by couples, in their forties or fifties, and apart from me only a few other younger guests stood out in the room. One of these young men, a Brazilian one, approached and said that he had discovered my nationality through the key ring unintentionally showing in the back pocket of my pants. Marcelo was there accompanying a friend, around Robert's age, and was living in the city for some years.

- I came here to study. I joined an internship program at a famous company for a few years, and now I work at a multinational. - he explained.

- That's great, congratulations. And how did you know about this party?

- John is my boss, and he invited me to this party. In fact, I expected it to be boring, but I'm finding it very cool.

- Well, me too. - I was not sure if *cool* would be the best definition for the party so far. But at least, it was being pleasant to be there.

We talked for a while, until Robert approached us.

- Hey, I found you! Are you running away from me, Vicente?

- Of course not. - I replied, a little bit embarrassed in front of Marcelo. - Robert, this is Marcelo, another Brazilian guy in New York.

- It is a pleasure to meet you. - he greeted him and turned to me. - Vicente, can I talk to you alone? - he looked bothered by something.

I excused myself from Marcelo and followed Robert to the balcony again.

- It's a fine apartment and a nice party, thank you for bringing me. - I said, being honest.

He didn't say anything back, just smiled at me.

- So... what did you want to tell me? - I asked, afraid of his gaze fixed on mine.

He kept smiling at me.

- Well... - he finally started to talk. - There is a reason why I asked you to accompany me to this party today. - and fell silent again, apparently waiting for me to question him what the reason was. Because I was silent too, he continued the talking. - Before I tell you the reason, I need to know something. Do you think I'm too old?

What kind of question was that?

- No, of course not. You're still young, stop it! - I said, trying to look relaxed. *What was I supposed to say to him?*

- And would you go out with a man around my age? - he asked, looking at me even more intently.

Did he know about Peter? Was he investigating me? Tinkering my stuff at home? Following me? It seemed ridiculous to have those thoughts, but I couldn't help it. I had always had a feeling that Robert was bipolar or something like that. I kept thinking for a while before answering.

- I think so, depending on my feelings about this man. - I decided to take the chance, because Peter was only a few years younger than Robert, and if he were to know about us, he couldn't use my own speech against me later.

Then something unexpected happened. Robert rested his punch glass on a high table next to us, took my glass out of my hand and placed it next to his. Then he held my hands tightly and looked me in the eye again, before continuing his speech.

- Vicente, I like you. And it's been awhile now. I don't know if you have noticed. But I have a great affection for you. And I wonder if you feel the same way about me. - he said, slowly.

I couldn't feel my hands, only his, very cold. *Was that real? I couldn't believe it.*

- Robert, I... - I started, not knowing how to continue. I waited for him to interrupt me, but he remained silent, really waiting for an answer. I wondered if this was the time to talk to him about Peter, even if I didn't feel like getting into that level of intimacy with him. So, I decided to be as honest as I could be with him. - I also have great regard for you, but I prefer that you remain just as my host.

He took his eyes off mine and looking down smiled slightly. I thought I saw a tear rolling down his cheek but didn't know how to react to it.

- Thank you for your sincerity, Vicente. This is one of the many reasons why I admire you. - he released my hands and handed me the punch back.

He liked me and was apparently into me. I had never thought of Robert that way. What I thought was a weird behavior could after all be just admiration for me. I was not prepared for this revelation. I always thought that the image he had of me was nothing more than a Brazilian guy who was renting a room in his apartment, and with a student life so troubled that it was impossible to find time to keep him company in activities around the neighborhood. Suddenly, his actions no longer seemed to be coming from a bipolar personality, but from someone afraid of a feeling for someone else. I didn't know what to think about Robert anymore. But the boredom I had felt for him in the past gave way to a certain compassion at that moment. Perhaps all he wanted was attention and to feel good about his sexual condition, currently hidden under a religious shell. In the end he still believed in some of the city's promises, although he said otherwise.

Robert excused himself to the restroom and walked away from me. I turned to the balcony window and faced Manhattan, still surprised by what had happened. The city had witnessed that scene, and suddenly its skyline seemed hard, severe. If I was right, that one had been another Robert's attempt to find love, and yet another failure. How many other people had gone through that situation before, and how many would still experience this kind of disappointment in the future? I wasn't specifically looking for love, but my relationship with Peter was getting stronger. Would I also have to pass the test?

New York was shining with the lights of its skyscrapers and looking more than ever like a concrete jungle.

CHAPTER XI

I had to travel but will be back before you leave for Brazil. Enjoy your first day of snow. R.

The note left under my bedroom door was another one that Robert had written for me and was the first thing I saw and read when I woke up the morning after the party. Daylight shone brightly through the windows. I opened the curtains and saw it. It was Christmas Day and it was snowing. A typical New York setting. In my mind and now in front of my very eyes.

I took a shower, dressed myself really quickly and went out. It was freezing, but the view of the street completely covered by a beautiful white layer made up for the uncomfortable sensation. There was nobody, if not me, contemplating that scenario. I took the subway towards Midtown.

Half an hour later I was entering Central Park, and I could see people of all ages playing with the ice, making snow angels on the floor, and sculpting snowmen of all sizes. Despite the strange sensation with which I had gone to sleep the night before, due to Robert's revelation at the party, at that moment I was happy, and I couldn't contain a broad smile.

I walked around the park a bit and sat on a bench near Bow Bridge. That bridge that had always been full of tourists the other times I had been in the park, that Christmas morning was empty. I looked at the trees, which were beginning to retain the snowflakes on their dry and twisted branches and found it a wonderful view. Suddenly, a different light towards the bridge caught my attention. I got up and followed it. The lake that ran below the bridge was freezing, and the clear snow reflected the sun that lit that winter sky. I followed the beam of light that was hitting the water, up to the sky, and what I saw was inexplicable. In a very clear blue sky, some clouds formed the letter V. V from Vicente. I was moved. When it comes to shape-interpretation of the clouds, everyone sees what they want, but it was clear to me that New York loved me too. That was the sign I was hoping to find. I stood there, admiring the sky, the snow, the park, the island.

The day passed, and I let myself be carried away by the new habits I had acquired. The city was all dressed up for the occasion for a few weeks but only that day I was able to look more closely at the details. Storefronts had changed, giving way to Christmas scenes with ornaments that almost completely covered their windows, showing animated dolls in familiar situations, or mannequins in luxurious clothes in sumptuous and cinematic settings. Gardens with pine trees, now covered with snow, followed the entire length of the wide avenues, and lampposts decorated in green, red and gold, were shining during the day and during the night. I had coffee in a Pret A Manger near Central Park, I walked down Fifth Avenue in the snow, I bought a thicker wool hat to shelter my head from the cold, I had lunch in a small restaurant on Seventh Avenue that I had gone to with Clara on other occasions, I went to Washington Square Park and let a crowd of people keep me company, I grabbed a cappuccino at Starbucks - a hot one, because my usual Frappuccino wouldn't work at that time, and then I went home. It was good to have that time exclusively for me, and to be able to do things I would never do in Brazil on Christmas Day. Nor better or worse things, just different ones. Activities and new hobbies that were mine. Mine and the city's.

The next day, I met Peter for lunch. We went to a cozy restaurant in West Village, with his friends, who were in town. A heterogeneous group of very nice people who made me feel at ease all the time. After a delicious dessert, Peter and I went to his apartment. The afternoon was filled with kisses and some ninety's movies.

- I'm leaving in a few days. - I said, making a sad face.

- Yes, the unfortunate date is approaching. I will miss you. - he hugged me. - Hey, we have to spend the New Year's Eve together!

I hadn't thought about what I would do on New Year's Eve until then, and the only invitation I had received was from some colleagues at Diplomacy, who were going to spend it in Times Square, to see the famous ball drop and then go to a nightclub party. Spending that occasion with Peter seemed more interesting for me, despite not knowing what the schedule would be.

- I would love to! - I cheerfully agreed.

Then he told me we would go to a party on the rooftop of his friend's apartment, to see the Central Park fireworks and after, a surprise would wait for me.

While he slept, I thought about us. I didn't want to overthink our relationship, so as not to run the risk of create expectations that could not be fulfilled, especially because I was leaving soon. But I was not able to avoid thinking about it. What we had was light, pleasurable, and adding to my experience in New York. We weren't officially dating, there were no plans for the future, but that didn't make our affair any less intense. I hadn't accessed G-Radar in a few weeks, and that was because I had no need to meet new people, new men. He was enough for me.

Watching Peter rest, and reflecting on everything, I found myself thinking that that man was who I would have liked to become, if I were to live there. That was the life I had always dreamed of. I fell asleep feeling happy.

The last days of classes at Diplomacy were basically filled with final exams, in which I performed very well, and also with goodbyes to students who, like me, would go back to their countries of origin at the beginning of the year. After the last class, in which we were given our certificate, I went to lunch with Akihiro and some other colleagues. I took the opportunity and officially said goodbye to everyone, after all we would not meet for the New Year's Eve. Like the other times, it was very nice, and especially relatable, as everyone commented on having learned a lot from the experience of living in another country and making new friends.

I started to feel nostalgic about the whole trip as the day of departing was approaching. Confused emotions were present in all my thoughts and actions, as I was proud of what I had accomplished and sad for having to leave.

I realized that Robert had arrived from his trip when I entered the apartment and he stepped forward to the door as soon as I closed it.

- Vicente, I bought you something. - he said, joyful.

- Oh, you didn't have to! We didn't agree on buying gifts for each other. - I tried to sound pleasant.

- I didn't *have* to, but I *wanted* to. - he said smiling.

We went to his room, and he handed me a square, red package. I opened the package and discovered a frame with a photo of me. On one of our trips to Fort Tryon Park, Robert and I had taken our respective cameras, to capture *the best New York's fall-to-winter landscapes*, as he had said to me at the time. I had just arrived in the city, and the trees were still losing the bright green of their foliage, beginning to turn into yellow tones. Without my knowledge, Robert had taken a picture of me while I was pointing my camera at a big tree, with the Hudson River in the background. I didn't know about this capture, but there it was, beautifully framed in dark elegant wood, and glass protecting the now-eternal scene.

- Robert, this is lovely. Thank you very much for the gesture. - I thanked him, with my voice shaking from holding my emotion.

We hugged. A tender hug.

I went back to my bedroom and kept looking to my photo a few more minutes. Seeing that image reminded me of when I had arrived in Manhattan, still very naïve about what I would find and about what Robert would mean to me. I remembered Tony Hendra's question in *Father Joe*. Now I could say that if a cat had kittens in the oven, they might not be biscuits, but they would know what being a biscuit *feels* like. At that point I could sense the power of experience. I could sense myself growing. I could understand empathy. And I could feel gratitude.

CHAPTER XII

Another marvelous apartment, elegantly decorated, with nice and cheerful people. A high floor overlooking part of the island, on a special celebration. It looked like an enhanced version of the Christmas party I had gone to with Robert a week earlier. Not so much for the location, or for the party itself. But for the company. This time I was comfortably side by side with Peter, and the occasion did not have a melancholy mood. On the contrary, I had more reasons than ever to celebrate. I had successfully completed my classes and was saying goodbye to the city that had taught me more about myself than I thought I could know. Also, the year was ending and giving way to a new one and I felt that all my travel goals had been completed.

Lucas no longer represented a possibility for me in the future, but a story that was over even before it had started. The distance had helped me and my new habits, including my affair with Peter, had changed what I nourished for Lucas. I no longer felt my mind getting excited or my heart beating faster at the memory of moments we had spent together, in a past that seemed distant in my head.

I had been by myself most of the time, enjoying pastimes without the company of other people and not feeling lonely. I found it liberating to be able to make small decisions without having to think about others' opinions when it wasn't necessary. I was choosing who would be part of my life without this being misinterpreted, and I was feeling wanted and loved by important people in my life, no matter how often I could see them or how far away they were.

A new Vicente was shaped.

As I prepared myself for the party, I realized how much I had grown up in that city, in the circumstances I had placed myself in, with the companies I had had, with the convictions I had obeyed. The environment had helped me, but the biggest credit was with me. I had been able to reflect when needed, stop when necessary, and act when inevitable. And all according to the level of maturity I had achieved. The best of all was feeling that no one could take that away from me, and that this new life would be taken with me wherever I went.

Peter was more attractive than ever, and like the time we met, all dressed in white. Particularly that night, I was more affectionate for him than ever and that helped me feel even happier. Midnight was approaching, and we all headed to a large balcony to wait for the countdown. Everyone was holding a glass with champagne in their hands and big smiles on their faces. I admired the incredible view of Manhattan that was even brighter and magical, lit by more lights than the usual.

- Vicente, I want this new year to be unforgettable for you. And for me. - said Peter.

- I want that too. - I agreed.

Someone from inside the apartment, running around the room, came screaming that the clock was marking ten seconds to the New Year, so we started counting backwards. Peter placed himself in front of me, took my hands, and closed his eyes, as if making a wish. I did the same, and envisioned positive things, just as I had done before turning the key to Robert's apartment on my first day in the city and also in St. Patrick's Cathedral months ago. Apparently, that ritual had worked the other times, so I repeated it.

At the end of the count, fireworks began to burst, shining different colors across the dark sky, making the city even brighter, almost imitating daylight. Peter pulled me closer and gave me a kiss. I succumbed to that delicious feeling, of being there, with him.

- Happy New Year, Peter!

- Happy New Year, Vicente!

After a delightful supper, we said goodbye to the others and left. Peter's apartment was not far from there and that turned out to be a positive fact, as it was impossible to get a taxi at that moment, so we walked. Arriving at the loft we went straight to the bathroom. Although Peter had a bathtub, we had never used it together. When I entered the room, I could barely believe how romantic a simple bath could look like. Since that night was obviously special, he had prepared a whole setting for us, managing to transform the moment into a relaxing massage session, with the ambiance lit by aromatic candles, and involved in soft music. After we had amazing sex and had a quick snack, the sky started to clear giving space to the morning clarity. Wrapped in a comfortable blanket and seated on one of the sofas in the living room, we kept looking out the large windows, admiring the view. Peter then turned to me, held my head softly with both of his hands and looked at my eyes with affection.

- Vicente, I have something to tell you.

- Yes? - I was suddenly a little apprehensive. I knew from experience that when someone started a speech like that, usually that didn't mean good news.

- Actually, it's not something to tell you. It's more of a request. - he said visibly, and as never before, nervous.

I kept looking at him.

- Do you want to be my boyfriend and come live with me?

My mind went from certainties to doubts in a matter of seconds.

I didn't know how to respond. I didn't see it coming. Although it seemed like the natural thing to happen in a normal reality, I had no expectations about it, as I had a date to leave the city. But at the same time, I would love to date Peter and move in with him. We got along so well together, and the new Vicente fit and deserved that relationship. I needed some time to think.

- How much time do I have, to think about it? - I asked, trying to look funny.

- As much time as you need... - he replied, uncertain.

- You remember I'm leaving tomorrow, right?

- Yes, I know that. But I couldn't let you go without trying to make you stay.

- You had never suggested that before...

- I know. I somehow thought it might not be the time. I don't even know if it is now, especially for you, because of your schedule to leave. But I would very much like you to think about it.

There it was. My inner sea, finally calm, had just been agitated again. When I thought I had answered all the questions I had collected during my stay in the city, my one hundred days on the island, when I felt confident that I had achieved all my goals and was certain about my choices, it seemed like a new big question mark had been placed in front of me, as a final test from fate before my departure.

- You bet I'll think about it. - I said, still in a light tone, trying uselessly to make that situation somehow relaxed.

He hugged me as if trying to convince me that we belonged together.

We went to sleep, but I was unable to remain in Peter's arms. He was calm and relaxed. My head kept going over all the events, looking for a sign that would define my response to that request.

At ten in the morning, I woke up and was alone in bed. I found a note next to me.

Had to go to the office for an emergency. Be back for lunch. XXX, Your Peter.

Although it was not explicitly written on that piece of paper, I knew that Peter expected me to have an answer for his request during that lunch. It would probably be our last time together before my departure. At least, that was what we had agreed before.

When Peter arrived two hours later, I still had a lot of doubts running through my mind. Countless. About my future, his expectations, and even how we would manage the visa issue for me to remain in the country.

- How do you expect our relationship to be? I mean, would I just move in with you to your loft? Wouldn't I disrupt your routine? Wouldn't it be best for me to have my own place? And what about the visa? What would I do for living to afford a place here? Or maybe we could try long distance relationship? I don't know... - I threw him a lot of questions when we were at the kitchen table, ready to eat.

- Vicente, calm down. - he began, after I ran over him with my questions. - We need to discuss these details carefully. But I think it would be more comfortable if you moved here, after all you love the city, right?

Yes, I loved New York, and I felt that the city loved me back. But I knew that this was not the same as loving Peter or being loved by him. Moving to the island didn't seem like a bad idea, on the contrary, it would be something I would love to consider. But for me, and not for another person. I was living something new and extremely valuable with Peter, and I would like to continue living it, but hearing him talk like that suddenly made me feel bad, as if I was being controlled by someone else. *More comfortable for you*, I thought. And although I had not yet planned my next year or defined my next goals in life, I knew that accepting something I was not sure because of another person's will would not match the new Vicente. Not in New York or anywhere else.

- Regardless of my answer, I have to leave tomorrow morning. You know that, right? - I asked him.

- I thought we could define some things now, and then decide the details. Vicente, I'm in love with you and I don't wanna lose you.

Hearing that took my breath away, made my heart beat faster.

- I think I'm in love with you too, Peter. - I said, with my eyes full of tears, about to fall down my face.

He asked me to stand and hugged me tight, starting to cry. I had never seen him so vulnerable.

- Say yes, Vicente. Please. Come live with me and I'll fix everything for us.

A continuation of my new lifestyle was being offered to me. Living with Peter would be wonderful. I would get to keep being the new Vicente, living in New York, with my whole future ahead of me. The new me. But it would not be fair to make that choice in those circumstances, because accepting that request would change the course of many other things in my story and also in his story. Impulsive love used to work well on movies, but I knew it didn't always work in real life. Furthermore, it seemed that he had already thought of everything, without even consulting me, and I suddenly felt like my freedom was being taken from me. When it came to plan romantic surprises and unexpected dinners there was no problem, but that decision in particular would give me few or no control over my future. Choosing to stay with him seemed hasty, going against everything I had achieved, all the maturity and experience I had earned. And I didn't have time to think it over.

I gently got out of the hug and looked him in the eyes. My chest was hurting.

- Peter, I can't accept it. - I said those words to him in the sweetest way I could. And I couldn't hold back my tears.

Peter hugged me again, wiped away his tears, and then looked at me tenderly.

- Vicente, you are handsome, intelligent, talented and would make any man the happiest guy in the world. Don't let anyone tell you otherwise. - he said.

- Thank you, Peter. For everything. - I was sobbing.

We stayed together for a few more minutes. We didn't eat, just stayed close to each other.

Leaving the loft was one of the most difficult moments of the entire trip, but I knew the new Vicente was leaving with me.

My ride back to Washington Heights that afternoon was filled with sadness. I would still visit the south of the island the next day, before heading to the airport. But I wouldn't see Peter anymore. Even with all the freedom and independence that I had achieved the last few months, knowing that someone there liked me so much made me torn.

CHAPTER XIII

I woke up early. It took me a long time to stand up from the big inflatable mattress I had called my bed for the last three months. Robert was still asleep when I left the apartment, heading for my last hours in New York. The New York that was even better and more real than the one I had imagined before arriving. Beneath two thick coats that kept me warm, was a t-shirt I had bought weeks before. A white short-sleeve t-shirt with the sayings *I Love New York*.

Walking the same avenues that I had walked, crossing the same streets that I had crossed, looking at the same skyscrapers I had looked at, everything seemed different. For the first time during the months I had lived there, it rained. I was saying goodbye to the island, and the island seemed to continue loving me, and sadly saying goodbye to me too. I sat at a table at a Seventh Avenue Starbucks, and once again reflected on everything that had happened in my life there.

On one hand there was Clara. During her time in New York, she had been what I could have been. Her trajectory could have been mine, with all the setbacks, if I had let myself succumb to the dazzles she had succumbed early on. Ironically, she had been *saved* by João, another Brazilian guy, not me. On the other hand, there was Robert, a man I could have turned into if I had given up of hope, and if I had run away hiding my feelings behind something else, like religion. He was what I could have become, had I not been able to get rid of things from the past. And I couldn't save Robert staying by his side. And then there was Peter. Peter had won me over for being authentic, in addition to his natural beauty and charm. The best thing about having him by my side was that I could consider him an example of success, a model for my life. I admired him. I knew that in his story he had dealt with many challenges and had put up a lot of work to achieve what he had achieved. That seemed very motivating to me. Based on what I had seen of him, I was encouraged to move on and have hope in the future. My future, wherever and with whomever it was going to be.

In the end, I had not been a hero, but I had learned that life is made of choices. And that it takes a lot of strength to make the right ones.

After a quick lunch at Pax in Times Square, I said goodbye to that crazy but loving neighborhood and headed north. I got home and finished packing my suitcases. When I closed the last one, Robert arrived home. He was carrying a package from his favorite bakery.

- Come have your last coffee with me! - he shouted from the kitchen.

I went to him and he was waiting for me with a hazelnut tart and a teapot on the stove.

- I'm boiling water for tea, have a seat. - he said.

- Robert, I'll need a taxi to go to the airport. Do you know a good company for me to call and ask for one?

- I've already ordered one for you. It must be here at five.

- Well, thank you very much! - I was surprised.

- I realized you would be busy thinking about other things, so I decided to help you. Try this pie, it is delicious.

I helped myself to a slice of it. After a few minutes of silence, he filled my cup with tea.

- Vicente, I want to thank you for not making a big deal about what I told you at that Christmas party.

- No problem, Robert. - I said, avoiding going too much into that matter. - I'm the one who need to thank you, for your hospitality.

- I did nothing more than a good host should do. - he smiled slightly. His blue eyes were bright, as in the good times we had spent together.

We finished the meal and the taxi arrived. Robert helped me down with my suitcases, two instead of one, as when I had arrived. The taxi driver was different from the one that has brought me to the building months before. Blond hair, green eyes and with a perfect English, he was a rare type of taxi driver in the city.

- Thank you very much for everything, Robert. - I hugged him. I felt that moment has brought us closer, in a good and unpretentious way.

I gave the apartment key back to him, and he started taking the keychain with the Brazilian flag off, to return it to me.

- No, I want you to have it. - I interrupted him.

- I will never forget the best guest I ever had. - he hugged me again, squeezing me tight.

I was happy with the way my story with Robert ended. Between good times and bad ones, he had been an important part of my story in that place.

I got in the cab, took a deep breath, and we left.

The rain that had stopped for a few hours, fell again and the scenery that I witnessed on the way to the airport was made of unusual images blurred by the dripping water on the windows of the car. Inside my mind, though, everything was clearer. Except for one thing. The new Vicente was still not sure if he had taken the right action, if he had made the best choice towards Peter. Only time would tell.

*"To live is the rarest thing in the world.
Most people exist, that is all."*

Oscar Wilde

ABOUT THE AUTHOR

Victor Gonçalves is a Brazilian writer interested in art, photography and cinema. He has held three photographic exhibitions and is the author of the novel *100 Dias Na Ilha*, the Portuguese version of *100 Days*.

With a degree in Communication, and MBAs in Trends & Innovation and Retail Management, he works with graphic design and retail consultancy, as well as maintaining the blog *O Mais Importante*, which talks about relevant aspects of daily life.